"You're here to be my eyes."

Drew had directed Sara to an isolated part of the reserve. "You accused me of never taking you on my forays into the wilderness," he continued. "Now you're the essential ingredient of an expedition. I brought you here to be my eyes. But I also brought you here to make love to you."

"Don't think you can seduce me," Sara retorted, "as you could when I was young and filled with ideas of romance."

"Didn't you return with the intention of helping me?" he asked smoothly. "Well, now's your chance. The good doctor suggested a second honeymoon, but neither of us wants that, do we? A short affair, however, might benefit us both."

"I have no intention of staying in this godforsaken place!"

"And I intend to convince you otherwise."

Wilderness Bride

Gwen Westwood

Harlequin Books

TORONTO • NEW YORK • LONDON
AMSTERDAM • PARIS • SYDNEY • HAMBURG
STOCKHOLM • ATHENS • TOKYO • MILAN

Original hardcover edition published in 1985
by Mills & Boon Limited

ISBN 0-373-02736-2

Harlequin Romance first edition December 1985

CHAPTER ONE

THE wedding tableau was the last and by far the most glamorous feature of the whole show. 'June Bride,' the announcer proclaimed in her most sexy, black velvet voice, and with that hundreds of rose petals, pink, yellow and white, floated on to the stage from their cleverly concealed places in the ceiling, somewhere up there among the glittering Venetian glass of the chandeliers, and the perfume that was being promoted showered out its flowerlike fragrance like deep red roses. Pairs of small girls, perfectly graduated in size, appeared as if by magic in their dresses of cream silk with huge puffed sleeves, their satin pumps making no noise but moving perfectly in time to the music of *Greensleeves*, their heads banded with wreaths of miniature pink roses and blue forget-me-nots.

How on earth had Madame managed to get them in Johannesburg in midwinter? thought Sara, standing in the wings, and already feeling wearied by the heavy weight of the voluminous folds of cream-coloured silks about her, supported as it was by layer upon layer of lacy petticoat and topped by a boned bodice. The jewellery felt heavy too, thousands of dollars' worth of diamonds adorning her neck, her wrists, and sparkling in her ears, for this was a show to promote the diamond business too, and Madame had been glad to come from Paris with all her best models to co-operate with the firm and promote her own successful dress designs in the glamorous setting of one of the newest hotels in Johannesburg.

This was the last show. The whole promotion had been a fantastic success. Madame had been very pleased, so pleased with Sara in fact that, as a special reward, she had suggested she should stay on for a month.

'You used to live in South Africa, didn't you?' she had said.

'Yes, I was brought up here.'

'So. You have friends here?'

'Not really. Not any more.'

'But you would like to stay and enjoy all this lovely sunshine for a while. I can spare you until the Autumn shows—but don't, I beg you, gain too much weight. All the fittings have been made already, and the dresses should be ready when we get back. You have been working hard, perhaps you deserve a little holiday. You are looking *un peu maigre*, a little too thin perhaps. You must stay the English type with a little dash of Paris, slim and elegant with those nice long legs but with complexion radiant and healthy like the best kind of English miss.'

'But I'm not really English, Madame,' Sara explained. 'I was born there, but I spent many years in Africa. My father worked here.'

'No matter. You look English. You have not this outdoor look that is fashionable here. Ah, these *jeunes filles*, these girls, they look glamorous now with their golden skins, but only wait twenty years and it will have turned to leather!'

'Not necessarily, Madame. I spent some years in wild dry country and my skin appears to have recovered.'

'You are one of the lucky ones, evidently,' observed Madame.

Not so lucky, Sara thought now, as she moved slowly forward to take her place in the centre of the stage. All the paraphernalia of a glamorous wedding was here except the bridegroom. The most important feature of the affair was missing. A little smile played on her lips as she heard the gasps of admiration at her appearance. People in the audience could have thought that so she would have looked in real life when she faced her lover at the altar dressed in these beautiful garments, sparkling with a tiara of diamonds in the gleaming red-gold of her hair, but her thoughts were far away. She was recollecting with a kind of twisted sadness the scene of her own wedding and contrasting it with the present rich pageantry. Drew hadn't wanted any fuss. They had been married in a register office and she had worn a safari suit that would be useful later.

'I don't want anyone else there,' he had said. 'It's you I want, only you. This is just something between you and me, and after that you'll be mine completely. No one must ever come between us.'

Even then he had been too possessive, but it had thrilled her, young as she was. She could remember still how he had looked at her then, even experience the strange trembling that she had felt when his eyes held hers in that commanding way, those aloof, gold-green, lion-like eyes that could become tender and melt her heart so that she would have done anything he wished. How young I was then, she thought. What a child! And yet it was only five years ago. It took me three years to become a successful model, but that was after my marriage, which only lasted two.

And yet we've never taken the final step of divorce. I suppose, while I'm here, I should try to arrange something, but I feel I couldn't bear to meet him again. I wonder if it could be arranged by remote control? Friends had been surprised that she had remained in this doubtful state, neither married nor single. 'You'll want to marry again some day,' they had said.

But I don't think I will ever meet anyone I could think of spending my life with, she thought. Never another Drew. It was such bliss while it lasted, even though we were totally unsuited, and at the end he had grown to hate me.

Sara tried to dismiss the thought of Drew from her mind and concentrated on managing the beautiful dress and guiding the small bridesmaids who were having a little difficulty with the long train. But it was odd how her thoughts would keep returning to him when she had tried, she believed successfully, to banish him from her mind in the last years. Her life had been so glamorous since she had become a leading model in one of the best known French houses that she had forsworn even the remembrance of him. At least that was the idea. It was only now that she had come back to Africa that memories were revived against her will.

And why should that be? This sophisticated round of work and pleasure in Johannesburg was an utter contrast to the life she had led with Drew. Even the air was different. It had a thin, diamond-bright quality that made you want to breathe quickly, to hurry from one engagement to another wearing beautiful clothes, to enjoy the parties given in their honour in the lovely houses on the outskirts of the City of Gold. Oh, no, her life had never been so luxurious before. The years of her marriage had been spent in the wilderness, for Drew was a game ranger in one of the toughest game reserves in Africa, the Etosha Pan in Namibia. Compared with this hot desert place, the reserves of South Africa with their luxurious tourist accommodation were gentle indeed. I must have been mad, Sara thought now, to believe I could make a success of a marriage with Drew, that dark stranger, obsessed with wilderness life, in such a place, But I was mad, wasn't I? Mad with love for him. Love that couldn't last.

The show was almost over now. The other models, dressed as wedding guests, promenaded upon the stage in a mock congratulation of the bride, and, in response to prolonged applause, Madame herself appeared and graciously accepted a bouquet. The lights in the auditorium grew brighter now, and it was then that Sara spotted him. Clive—Clive Deakin. Good grief, what could he be doing here? But there he sat, looking larger than life on one of the small gilt chairs, a weighty bull, not exactly in a china shop but as out of place in this scented place devoted to clothes and perfume and jewels as that animal would have been. She remembered his bright blue eyes, his ruddy cheeks, his reddish hair, as if she had only seen him yesterday. He had been devoted to Drew like some faithful dog, but he had always been good to her too. Even in those last dark days he had never taken sides, had even tried in his clumsy way to patch things up between them. But what was he doing here? Could he have brought a message from Drew? Oh, no, that was impossible. He must have seen the report of their show in the newspapers and came out of curiosity or kindness. But it was the last place in which Sara would have expected to see him.

The show was finally over and at last the wedding dress with its intricate fastenings of hundreds of buttons and satin loops had been taken off and the diamonds safely locked away. Sara removed her stage make-up and put on a fine wool grey dress, intricately cut but of a deceptive simplicity, and a short silver mink coat against the chill winds of the High Veld winter. She and the other models were staying at a smaller hotel down the road. But as she stepped out of the hot scented air of the dressing room and made her way to the foyer, Clive was waiting for her.

'Clive, how good to see you!' she exclaimed. 'Did you enjoy the show?'

'Hi, Sara, long time no see. The show? Oh, yes, it was pretty good, I guess, if you go for that kind of thing. First time I've seen one. I don't go for these modern racy set-ups, but I must say you looked great in that wedding outfit. You look great now.'

'Thank you, Clive. What are you doing in Johannesburg? You always said you hated it.'

'I do. Look, Sara, could we have a drink together? I've got something to tell you.'

His expression was very serious and Sara was surprised that suddenly an icy splinter seemed to enter into her heart.

'It's Drew, isn't it?' she said quickly. 'Something's happened to him? He isn't . . .?'

She felt Clive's great hand close over her arm.

'No, Sara, he's fine. At least . . . not exactly. Come, let's sit down somewhere and order a drink, then I'll tell you why I've come.'

Sara let herself be led over to a small table in a tiny intimate bar. She asked for tomato juice while Clive ordered a brandy. She was still trembling a little and felt annoyed that this should be so.

'Whatever you have to tell me, Clive,' she said now, 'anything to do with Drew is no concern of mine. We definitely agreed to separate all of three years ago—you know that. I've put all that part of my life behind me.'

'I understand that,' said Clive. 'No, that's not true—I never will understand why you two parted. You seemed so happy at first. No two people could have been happier.'

'At first, yes. But, Clive, it was only physical attraction, although at the time I believed it was love. We were too different to make a go of it. Drew was difficult, moody, jealous even, and the place was so awful, all that dust and heat.'

'You would never get Drew to see that,' Clive commented. 'Being a game ranger is his life.'

'But being a game ranger's wife wasn't my life. No, Clive, it just didn't work. It's best forgotten.'

'But you are still married to Drew, aren't you, Sara?'

'Unfortunately, yes. I never seem to have got round to doing anything about it.'

'Isn't that because you don't want to?' he queried.

'No, Clive, no! I tell you my life with Drew is over, has been over for three years.'

'But you're still his wife,' said Clive, 'and a wife's place is by her husband's side when he's in trouble.'

'Whatever trouble Drew has, I think he can look after himself,' Sara said coldly. 'He certainly doesn't need me.'

'Oh, but he does, believe me, Sara,' he said seriously.

'What are you trying to tell me?'

'Drew's in a pretty desperate state, Sara. Something has happened to him that, according to the specialists, was a chance in thousands. He had a routine injection against cholera when he was due to go to Mauritius a couple of months ago and it affected the optic nerve. He has great difficulty with his sight. Apparently everything is shadowy. He can't see colours—everything appears black and grey. There's a risk that eventually he may become blind.'

'Oh, no, Clive, I can't believe it!' she gasped, horrified.

'I'm afraid it's true. It came on him quite suddenly with hardly any warning. In Mauritius he noticed that the lights in the place where he stayed seemed rather dim, but he put it down to the fact that the chalets were rather primitive and the lighting more so. But he couldn't see the horizon very distinctly and colours seemed to be not as bright as usual. He had spent some days by the sea and thought this might be the dazzling effect of the white sands. However, when he came back and started to drive his car in Johannesburg, he couldn't see the kerbs of the roads, and the traffic lights all appeared to be a kind of uniform grey.'

'What happened then?'

'He immediately went to a doctor, who sent him to a specialist. At first they thought he must be suffering from some kind of brain tumour and subjected him to all kinds of horrible tests. Sara, I tell you, he's been through hell—so much so that he's become impatient with doctors and hospitals, and because they don't seem to be able to do any more for him and keep sending him to different specialists to try to solve the problem, he finally threw in his hand and insisted on returning to Etosha.'

'But you said it was because of the injection. Surely they must have realised that?'

'Not at first. They still can't positively account for it, but they think that must be the most likely cause. As I said before, it's a chance in a million that this should have happened.'

Sara was silent for a few moments. The tomato juice tasted acid and bitter on her tongue.

'I can't imagine that he would want me around if it's like you say,' she said finally.

I can't imagine him needing me at all, she thought. That was the whole trouble. Drew always seemed so self-sufficient in his life in the wilderness that there was too little place for me. But I can't bear to think of him being made helpless.

'Maybe he doesn't want you, but, Sara, he needs you. He's been wonderful. He has plenty of courage, as you know, and I've done my best for him, but it isn't enough.'

'What makes you think I could do anything?' she asked.

'Because you're the woman he loved. The only woman. Maybe you could reconcile him to the sort of life he'll have to lead from now on.'

'I notice you put it in the past tense,' said Sara. 'Clive, whatever love he had for me disappeared before we parted. In the end he seemed to hate me.'

'You mean that business with Brad Kavanagh? But everyone knew that was ridiculous.'

'Everyone but Drew. No, Clive, I'm sorry about this, but I couldn't stand to meet Drew again after all those ugly scenes. He was too jealous, too possessive. I should have known how he would be from the beginning, but I was so young.'

And I adored him, she thought.

'In any case, Brad Kavanagh is no longer there,' said Clive. 'He works in some reserve in another part of Africa now. You need never see him again.'

The business with Brad had been the final straw. Brad had been handsome, any tourist's dream of a game ranger, and from the first he had paid Sara too much attention and aroused Drew's enmity. He and Drew had been like two male lions fighting for dominance in the pride, but Drew's jealousy had been unfounded and unjust. He had come back unexpectedly from a safari and found Brad in the house with Sara, who had been trying to fend off his attempts at lovemaking. The situation had looked suggestive and Sara had been too proud to offer any excuses or explanation. Besides, she thought now, it was only the final break in a marriage that had been doomed since the beginning.

'It was all hopeless,' she said to Clive now. 'I was a fool to marry him, but I was so in love. I might have known it wouldn't work. All of life that I knew was being brought up in a luxurious house in Cape Town with indulgent parents, then winning that beauty contest and getting work as a model. You must admit it was a poor start for life in the bush, wasn't it?'

'It was when your parents were killed in that plane crash that you decided to marry, wasn't it?'

'Yes. They hadn't thought Drew suitable when they met him, he was so much older and already obsessed with wild life, but I would have been willing to go against their wishes even if that hadn't happened. When they were gone there seemed to be no one else in the world to turn to except Drew. He was wonderful to me then.'

'So why can't you be wonderful to him now?' urged Clive.

Sara was suddenly overwhelmed with memories of those first days of their marriage. She had worshipped Drew, had been willing to go anywhere to be near him. *I owe him something at least,* she thought.

'If you think it would do any good,' she said slowly and reluctantly, 'I'll come to see him. When do we start?'

Clive's great hand came down to enclose hers and give it a mighty hurting squeeze.

'That's my girl! I've booked two places on this evening's plane to Windhoek and tomorrow we'll drive to Etosha. We'll be there by sunset.'

'You were so sure I'd come?'

'I didn't think you'd let me down. How are you fixed with Madame what's-her-name?'

'I'm surprised you even consider that,' Sara said wryly, 'You're being so high-handed with me.'

'I confess I'm just thinking of Drew. It's on my mind all the time.'

'Well, my side of it doesn't seem to be worrying you,' she said, 'but if you want to know Madame offered me a vacation in Africa before I have to return to Paris. She said one month.'

'So that's all right, isn't it?'

'I suppose so. I'm giving up the first vacation I've had in three years to go to that horrible place where we both know I'll be unwelcome, but you've bullied me into it.'

'You'll see it's for your own good, yours and Drew's,' Clive assured her.

'I very much doubt it,' said Sara.

Their plane ascended above the glittering city as the sun set in golden splendour beyond the silver white mountains of the mines dumps.

'I hope you realise,' Sara told Clive, 'that you've cheated me of a splendid party, the grand farewell jamboree for Madame given by the diamond firm. I was due to wear a million dollars' worth of jewels tonight.'

'I don't think you'll miss them,' said Clive.

'You're very hardhearted. Only think, I could have been in Cape Town tomorrow and I'd been offered a cottage at Hermanus for a month, complete with cook and all mod. cons. And now, in place of the beautiful Cape, you offer me Etosha.'

'Etosha and Drew,' said Clive.

'That's what's worrying me. I don't know which prospect scares me most.'

But I do really, she thought. Oh, heavens, why did I let Clive persuade me to come? How can I face Drew after all these years of silence?

'Does he know I'm coming?' she asked Clive now.

'Of course not. It's going to be a glorious surprise for him.'

'I don't see where the glory is coming from,' She said ruefully. 'I should think I'm the last person he'll want to see in the circumstances.'

'You're too hard on yourself,' Clive told her. 'He'll be pleased you've come. Even if he's never admitted it, there must have been times when he regretted parting from you. And surely you've missed him occasionally, Sara?'

'I told you before, I've refashioned my mode of living. Drew has no part in the life I lead now.'

'Do you like that kind of life?'

'Of course,' said Sara defensively. 'What girl wouldn't enjoy living in Paris, wearing some of the world's most beautiful clothes, meeting interesting people, eating at gorgeous restaurants?'

'And you don't regret giving up the life you had with Drew in the wilderness? At one time I thought it suited you very well.'

'Perhaps it did for a while, but then Drew was sent on all those safaris and I wasn't allowed to join him, and the place began to get me down—the dust, the heat, being confined to the barricaded camps, the noises of the animals. I guess I was just yellow. When I was left alone I was just plain scared.'

'You were very young, remember. When I first met you you looked like a girl just out of school, with your huge violet eyes and long shining hair. Do you remember you used to do it in pigtails?'

'That was to keep cool,' she explained.

I mustn't start remembering, she thought. I must only remember how things were at the end, not how it was at the beginning. I mustn't remember those nights with Drew, the long starlit nights when I'd be awakened by the lions' roaring and we would make love with the rhythmic sound of the fan on the ceiling whirring overhead. The mosquito net draped the bed so that we seemed to be in a world of our own, a gauzy unreal world where only Drew and myself and the passionate response of our bodies existed. That world was an illusion that was soon broken. Oh, what am I doing here, flying towards a place I grew to hate, to a man who I'm sure grew to hate me? She had thought that when she had her month's leave she would fly to Cape Town, hire a car, renew her acquaintance with the lovely scenery of the Cape, visit the wine farms, enjoy the sunshine having lunch under the oaks, see the gracious white old Dutch farmsteads against their background of blue mountains, bathe in the Indian Ocean, surfing on the blue and white breakers.

But here she was flying above the desert country of Namibia where rivers only existed for most of the year as a sandy track outlined by scrub, where the desert was bounded by the icy seas of the Atlantic that only seals could really appreciate.

Now they were touching down at Windhoek, the

capital of Namibia, where they were to stay the night.
To Sara, used to the sparkling hustle of Paris, it seemed
a sedate provincial town, with wide streets and modern
buildings except for a few churches and other old
buildings of German origin left over from their colonial
occupation. The hotel, however, had sophisticated
showcases with numerous souvenirs for the tourist—fur
coats, rugs of zebra and lion skins, semi-precious stones
made up into exciting jewellery, tiger's eye, rose quartz,
chalcedony, malachite and amethyst, all mined in this
arid country. Strolling in the main street with Clive
after dinner, Sara saw Herero women, made even larger
and taller by their vivid Victorian costume and
colourful turbans. She remembered that she had been
so fascinated by them when she first came here that she
had bought a doll dressed in their distinctive costume,
and Drew had laughed indulgently at her enthusiasm.

He had bought her a necklace of polished amethyst
stones, telling her to wear it always because it matched
her eyes. It suited me better than diamonds, she thought
now. I wonder what happened to it? Where is it now?
Somewhere hidden away with the pitifully few souvenirs
of the years of our marriage, I guess.

They breakfasted at seven to try to avoid some of the
day's heat, but Sara knew this was rather a forlorn
hope, since the journey would take several hours. It
would have been quicker by plane, but that would have
meant chartering one, and in any case Clive had left his
car in Windhoek.

'I like to spend a few days here occasionally when I
have the chance,' he explained. 'To hit the high spots a
bit, have a few more beers than usual, go to a rugby
match, meet the boys.'

Sara smiled at Clive's idea of a hectic time, and yet
she remembered how thrilling she had thought it on
those very few times when Drew had brought her into
town and they had dined and danced at some hotel.
Once a year the town came alive when there was the
German beer festival, accompanied by all kinds of
gaiety and entertainment, and that had been exciting.

Out of Windhoek, the road was good, making its way through country covered with shrub, a wilderness of thorn trees with their strange flat tops, mopane with red and yellow leaves and tamboti, which Sara remembered as the jumping bean tree because the fruit often contained the larva of an insect which made it jump into the air. What silly things stay in one's memory! she thought. Sometimes there were gigantic ants' nests, six feet tall, pointing a finger at the burnished sky.

There was plenty of time for memories to come flooding back along this straight monotonous road. I was a fool to come, she thought. What can I do for Drew, except upset him? At Okahandja they stopped for a drink and a sandwich, then onwards into the heat of the afternoon, past Otjiwarango and then to Outjo, all small towns set down for some trading purpose in this semi-desert, this country of dust and heat. After Outjo the road was untarred, made up of gravel that produced a storm of fine grey dust in a cloud behind the car. Now Sara knew they were getting nearer to their destination.

'Where exactly are we going to, Clive?' she asked. 'Where is Drew staying now?'

'He's staying at Okaukuejo, because, as you may remember, there's a waterhole there in the camp. This sight thing doesn't seem to worry him as much at night—I suppose because at night it doesn't matter so much if everything appears colourless. He says the elephants at the waterhole are the only animals which appear completely natural. He chose to stay there because, if he can't sleep, he can stay by the waterhole and know by the sounds what's going on.'

'Is it as bad as that?' asked Sara apprehensively.

She felt appalled to think of Drew staying sleepless at the waterhole hoping to recognise the animals by sound and not by sight—he who, when she had been with him, had astonished her by the way his keen eyesight picked out the smallest insect, the most distant cheetah that to her unaccustomed eyes blended in with the background of dry grass and russet leaf.

'It's bad, Sara, and it may get worse. God knows what's to happen to him. You know he had no time for the routine office work. He was always impatient of the need for tourists, thinking that the work with the animals was of paramount importance. He always preferred going into the bush, going on safari, to any other kind of pandering to the general public, but now he's stuck in the camp, not allowed to go out. How can we let him risk his life going into the bush when he can't see clearly, when all around him everything is grey? And yet it's killing him, Sara. If he has to leave the service, and be invalided out, what's left for him?'

Yes, that was all he ever wanted, thought Sara. He expected his wife to be as enthralled with wild life as he was. And yet he would never let me go with him on the dangerous trips, the ones that took him away for weeks. He didn't think I had the courage. If I had insisted . . . but it only led to arguments. I never really got to share that side of his life. Maybe that's where we went wrong.

Those were the unbearable times, alone under the mosquito net in the breathless dark, hearing the screeching squabbling of ·baboons and the terrible demonic laughter of the hyenas. Alone like that, I would forget those other nights, the golden moonlight flooding into the whitewashed room, his eyes mysteriously dark, his lips hard and demanding upon the softness of my breasts, and my body soft and pliant, responding to his every touch. At those times I was entirely his, but was he ever entirely mine? No. Part of him was always away in the wilderness. Part of him could never be tamed.

The hundred odd miles from Outjo seemed to go all too quickly to Sara. What am I doing here? she thought as they approached the gate of the reserve. Why have I come? What good can I do? Drew won't want me near him—I know it.

It was October, still the dry season, but nearing summer, the same time of the year, Sara remembered, as when she had first arrived here. She saw again the dry flat plains covered with bush, the colourless vegetation,

the strawlike grass, tawny lion-coloured country with
not a touch of green. What had she expected that first
time? Her only previous experience of a game reserve
had been of the ones in Zululand, Umfolosi and
Hluluwe. In these places there was wilderness, certainly,
but green and flourishing, full of blossoming trees and
shrubs. This dry fierce country did not seem made for
man to live in. To Sara it had always seemed wild and
terrifying.

Drew had explained that at one time it was thought
there had existed a great inland lake made by the
Kunene river, but the course of the river had changed
and, as a result, the lake dried up and the Etosha Pan
was formed, a great wide floor of sand, barren of any
plant life but surrounded by plains with grass and
shrubs where countless animals lived.

'You remember all this?' asked Clive now, waving to
the barren landscape.

'Oh, yes, very well,' Sara replied.

This country, strange and wild, different from
anything she had ever known, seemed to close in on her
as it had done before. And yet, and yet ... *I had
forgotten there was a certain beauty here,* she thought.
The heat of the afternoon had slackened as the sun
moved westwards and a group of zebra tossed their
heads impatiently as they processed in single file to a
waterhole. Even the dust from the car was bathed in a
rosy haze and now it seemed quite natural that the grass
should be gold instead of green.

'Here's Okaukuejo,' said Clive. 'Drew's going to get
the surprise of his life, you bet!'

'You sound very optimistic, Clive,' sighed Sara. 'It's
more than I am.'

'Do you want to have a shower and so on before you
meet him?' asked Clive.

So he wasn't as confident as he sounded. Now he had
accomplished his mission, was he chickening out of
facing Drew's wrath?

'I'll meet him now,' said Sara firmly. 'That's what
I've come for, isn't it?'

I can hardly turn around and run the hundreds of miles back to Windhoek, can I? she thought.

'Let's get this over,' she told Clive. 'But promise me if it doesn't work, you'll find some way to get me back to Johannesburg.'

'Of course,' said Clive. 'But believe me, it's going to work. You can bet on that.'

'I'm not going to bet you anything, because I have a feeling you would lose the bet. Now take me to him.'

'One thing I can bet on—that he'll be by the waterhole at this time of day.'

The sun was setting rapidly now glamorising the whole camp with a glowing gold. It was all set out with square thatched huts for the visitors and central living quarters for the staff. Away from the paved pathways one's feet sank into soft sand; Sara felt it shifting in her thonged sandals as she followed Clive to the waterhole on the extremity of the camp.

Whatever has happened to him now, he doesn't mean anything in my life any more, she told herself firmly.

'There, I told you he'd be here,' said Clive. 'I'll slip away tactfully, shall I?'

He's scared, thought Sara, but so am I.

Between the edge of the camp and the waterhole there was a strong mesh fence and on the camp side of it there was a sturdy stone wall with a wide flat top where a spectator could rest his arms, possibly in order to steady his binoculars to get a better view. But at this time of day, the tourists were getting ready for the evening meal after their excursions into the reserve, and there was only one person standing alone beside the wall. Drew. From the back he looked just the same. Sara noticed with beating heart his tall lithe frame, the breadth of his powerful shoulders contrasting with the whipcord slenderness of his hips and thighs in the corded jeans. As she approached him she tried to walk softly and she thought that the soft sand had muffled her footsteps, but immediately he turned, and the blank but alert gaze of his golden green eyes was like the wary look of an animal caught unawares, hostile and dangerous.

'Who is it?' he asked.

Although obviously he was trying to use a normal voice to someone he probably thought was one of the tourists, he moved uneasily, like a horse that is a little wild towards strangers. Sara had been determined that whatever had happened to Drew she would try to be unaffected by it emotionally, but now a terrible shaft of pain seemed to pierce her somewhere in the region of her heart.

I mustn't weep, he'd hate it, she told herself.

'It's me—Sara,' she said softly.

'Sara! Good grief, I must be dreaming!'

His hands came forward and she felt them grasp her shoulders, then his fingers were on her face tracing the line of her cheek, then the soft curve of her mouth.

'I'm not a dream,' she whispered. She was shaken to the core by the effect his hands could still have upon her even now. 'Yes, it is Sara. Not a dream this time.'

For a moment she thought she glimpsed a trace of the tenderness she had once known—and then she knew she had imagined it, for he dropped his hands and went to stand some yards away from her, saying in a rough voice, 'What the hell brings you here, Sara?'

'I was in Johannesburg doing a fashion show. I met Clive and he told me what had happened. He thought I should come.'

'So it was Clive's idea—I might have known it! He's acted like an over-conscientious sheepdog ever since this happened.'

'He's very concerned about you, Drew,' she pointed out.

'Yes, he's a good fellow, there's no one like him. But he sometimes gets mad ideas, and this is one of them. How could he think I would want you to see me like this?'

Across the stretch of water a kudu bull stood majestically on its own, its magnificent spiral horns silhouetted against the red glow of the setting sun, and Sara thought that there was a kind of resemblance between that beast and the man at her side, so aloof and so separate.

'I think Clive's idea was that since we'd been important to each other and had known each other well, I might be of some help to you now.'

'I don't need any help, least of all from you, Sara,' said Drew coldly, 'We walked out of each other's lives all of three years ago. Whatever I have to face now, I have to do it alone.'

'Sometimes you can see things more clearly if you discuss your problems with another person. I mean . . . I mean, Drew . . .'

Sara realised that she had blundered by putting it this way. Only too well she remembered that sardonic laugh.

'If only it were that simple! Talk it all over with your wife whom you haven't seen for three years and your sight will miraculously return!'

'You know I didn't mean that. I admit I could have phrased it better. But, Drew, it does help to feel you aren't entirely alone at a time like this,' she urged.

'Oh, Sara, you're wasting your time by coming here. Anything I have to face I can do alone. I don't need anyone's pity, least of all yours. I expect Clive's intentions were good—they always are, the big blundering idiot that he is. What good did he think he could do by bringing you here? Did he hope to achieve some grand reconciliation just because I'm losing my sight? If we couldn't keep our marriage together before when I lived my normal life, I can't see how we could come together in these circumstances.'

Sara felt again the indignation she had always suffered when he argued with her.

'Who's mentioned such a thing as a reconciliation?' she demanded. 'Clive thought I might be of some help to you, but I certainly have no wish to start our marriage again. I was in Johannesburg and had been given a couple of weeks' leave when I met Clive, and it seemed a good opportunity to come back and see you. Even if it hadn't been for your mishap, it would seem sensible to get in touch with you. We should eventually clear up our situation, I suppose.'

'Oh, so that's it! You didn't come because Clive appealed to your better nature but because you're wanting a divorce. Tell me, who's the lucky man?'

'Lucky man?' she queried. 'Oh, you mean . . .'

'There must be someone after all this time. Remembering your passionate nature maybe there've been several. But now, I suppose, you've met someone you intend to marry.'

'Perhaps I have, but we've been apart for a long time. Anything I've done in those years needn't concern you, need it, Drew?'

His eyes were alive with their old fire. It was difficult to believe that he could not see her properly, that it was only a vague shadow that he took hold of now. Sara felt his arms around her, his hands seeking the gentle lines of her body that had once been so well known to him. Then his mouth came down upon hers, swift and sure as it had always been. She tried to keep stiff and unresponsive, but his mouth upon hers demanded surrender, and she felt the soft curves of her lips parting under the fierce onslaught of his kiss.

'Does he know how to kiss you as we did? Is he as good at making love to you? Fortunate fellow, he can see those violet eyes. Do you look at him with that same expression of absolute surrender that you had for me?'

'And if I do,' demanded Sara, 'what has it to do with you any more? Let me go, Drew. It seems nothing can tame you.'

'Not even the threat of blindness, Sara. So don't feel any pity for me. You've chosen to come here, or Clive persuaded you. But if you came on an errand of mercy, you're wasting your time. On the other hand, even if you came to ask for a divorce, you haven't got it yet— so don't forget that while you're here you are still my wife!'

CHAPTER TWO

SHE had drawn away from him and they were standing apart but facing each other when she heard this voice in the background.

'Oh, there you are, Drew, I've just got back. I got some wonderful photographs, and I came straight to you because I knew you'd want to hear all about it.'

Sara turned to see the owner of the assured, self-confident voice and saw a woman who matched it, tall with a lovely opulent figure, slender waist in the close-fitting sand-coloured slacks, perfect breast outlined by the clinging T-shirt, arms and neck and beautiful face all the same uniform colour of gold, eyes of a huge melting brown and hair, in spite of the heat, flowing freely in a dark waterfall over her shoulders.

She looked at Sara with an expression of arrogant curiosity. Drew's expression had changed subtly from that of aggression and anger that he had shown towards Sara a few moments ago. Now it seemed that his face turned towards this beautiful stranger was alive and interested.

'Glad you had a good day,' he said. 'I thought about you a lot.'

'Yes, that route you planned for me and my crew was the tops. Sorry you wouldn't come. Another time, maybe.'

Drew shrugged his shoulders.

'At present I'd simply be a hindrance and you know it. Maxine, let me present a visitor. Maxine is a photographer making a book about Etosha. This is Sara, my ex-wife—Maxine Galbraith.'

Sara saw an expression of amazement pass like a shadow across the lovely face. So I'm his ex-wife now, am I? she thought. And a moment ago I was still his wife. Well, well!

Drew turned to Sara.

24

'You didn't tell me whether you were still using my surname, Mannion?'

'No, I'm not,' Sara told him flatly. 'For professional purposes I use my maiden name. I'm known as Sara Haden.'

'Sara has made a success of her modelling career,' Drew told Maxine, 'She works in Paris. That's so, isn't it, Sara?'

'Yes,' Sara agreed. 'But how did you know?'

'Oh, I have some kind of bush telegraph. No, as a matter of fact, someone left behind a copy of some magazine and Clive noticed a photograph of you in it. He brought it to me like a faithful dog retrieving a bird. Rather an extinct one, I'm afraid.'

'So what brings you here?' demanded Maxine.

I could ask the same about you, thought Sara. The possessive way this woman was hanging on to Drew's arm was beginning to get on her nerves.

'I've been doing a promotion of French fashions and perfume in Johannesburg,' she answered. 'Clive happened to meet me and persuaded me to spend a few days' leave here.'

Sara saw the other woman's eyes look over her with ill-concealed scorn.

'I wouldn't have thought this kind of place was particularly your scene,' she observed.

'Sara has come on an errand of mercy or an errand of necessity, depending how you look at it,' Drew told her. 'She won't be staying long, will you, Sara?'

'I hardly think I shall,' Sara agreed.

She was furious with Drew and with this woman. And she didn't feel too kindly towards Clive either. When she saw him she would tell him what she thought of him persuading her to come here when he must have known that Drew was involved with this ... this ... female serpent who was winding her tanned arms around Drew's and drawing him away from Sara.

'How about that date we made to have dinner together tonight?' asked Maxine. 'I suppose now you'll be dining with Sara?'

'Certainly not,' said Drew. 'Our date still stands. Clive brought Sara here, they can have dinner together. I expect you would prefer that, Sara?'

'It's immaterial to me,' said Sara, trying to sound casual.

'And, Maxine, perhaps you could help fix up a chalet for Sara's use if Clive hasn't already done so,' added Drew.

'Willingly. Come along, Sara, the camp's pretty full, but we'll find a room somewhere for you. I'll see you later, Drew.'

Sara did not speak as she followed Maxine's straight back and flowing silky hair towards the huts, and when Maxine turned to speak to her, there seemed to Sara to be an expression of triumph in the girl's huge shining eyes.

'I hope you don't mind, but I'm the only person Drew will consent to see him eat. It's a bit of a struggle, you know, and he hates to make mistakes before strangers.'

Well, I suppose you could call me that, thought Sara. Come to think of it, we have been strangers for three years. But all the same it had given her a strange pang to hear the other girl speak so possessively of Drew. Obviously she was determined to exclude Sara from renewing any relationship. But I don't want to renew a relationship with Drew, do I? Sara asked herself. What am I doing here at all? I was a fool to come. She waited while Maxine went over to the office to find out what chalet could be allotted to her.

'As I told you, the camp's rather crowded right now, but I've managed to find a place for you. It's a bit isolated, but you won't mind that, will you? After all, you did spend two years here before, I understand. You must know what it's like—not exactly the Ritz, but you aren't in Paris now.'

The small round thatched hut Maxine showed her was far away from the main buildings of the camp, and Sara wondered whether Maxine had arranged this to make things as uncomfortable as possible during what she now thought would be a short stay.

'Where is Drew staying?' she asked.

'He's in the staff quarters, of course. He would hardly be in the tourist accommodation.'

Sara knew that the staff quarters were some distance away from the place that had been allotted to her. It was obvious that Maxine was not going to allow her to have much contact with Drew if she could help it.

She glanced at the other girl as Maxine lingered in the doorway. She had a beautiful figure, broad-shouldered, but with a slender waist and large perfect bosom and long strong legs like some Roman goddess. She looked the ideal person for this kind of life, strong yet beautiful and utterly confident in herself.

'Sara—I hope you don't mind if I call you that—do you mind if I say something to you?' asked Maxine.

'Feel free.'

'I don't know what Clive's idea was in bringing you here. I suppose his intentions were fine, but believe me, it's not going to do any good—in fact I would think you could do Drew quite a lot of harm.'

'Indeed?' drawled Sara.

'This has all been a terrific shock to his system,' Maxine explained. 'Of course, he's been wonderful about it. He's so courageous. I guess someone who hasn't been with him, someone who doesn't know him as I do, can't appreciate how marvellously he's faced up to all this, but obviously your presence must be a disturbing factor. I tell you, Sara, he doesn't need any more emotional upset at the moment.'

'I don't fancy there'll be any emotional upset, Maxine. Clive asked me to come because he was worried about him. He thought, mistakenly it seems now, that I could be of some help.'

'I'm glad you agree with me. So you won't be staying, will you?'

Sara looked at the eager triumphant expression on the face of the other woman and thought, why should I take it for granted that I can be of no help to Drew? That kiss had shaken her more than she cared to admit. Her body had betrayed her, responding to the memories that his hands, his mouth had recalled. But no, those memories were too dangerous now. And Maxine was obviously sure that she was the woman in possession.

'Clive said he could arrange for me to go back to Windhoek if I decided not to stay here,' she told Maxine. 'I'll discuss it with him at dinner.'

'I knew you'd see it my way,' said Maxine, and, with a swing of her curving hips in their tight camel jeans, she headed for the door and across the waste of soft sand that separated Sara's chalet from the main camp. In the rapidly deepening dusk, Sara thought Maxine in her dark gold outfit and with her mane of hair was like some lioness that knows no other animal can hope to rival it.

The shower in the small bathroom worked well and, refreshed and revived, she put on a dress of white voile with small sprigs of flowers, pink, blue and yellow. Most of her Paris dresses were too sophisticated for life in the wilds, she thought, but this dress was suitable, with its tiny shoestring straps that left her shoulders bare in the dry heat of the night.

'You look great,' Clive told her when she met him in the main building. Tables were set under a thatched roof that had walls of netting to let in the air but keep out the moths and flying beetles that were stunning themselves against the mesh. At one end there was a bar with curving counter and wooden stools, and many of the visitors were sitting there recounting their day's adventures.

'After this month we'll be left in peace,' Clive told her. 'We close the park to tourists for the summer months. It's too hot, and of course it's the rainy season. The roads become impassable then. The mosquitoes breed and we still get malaria here. It can be prevented now, of course.'

'Yes, I remember it well. How I hated having to take those malaria tablets! They always made me feel sick.'

'I expect they've been improved since then. If you have to take them this time you won't feel a thing.'

'Good heavens, Clive, I don't expect to stay here

until the rainy season!' exclaimed Sara. 'In fact, I want to remind you of your promise that if I wanted out straight away you would see to it.'

'Surely you don't mean that?' Clive's kind face was a study of dismay.

'Certainly I do. When you were so persuasive in Johannesburg, you omitted to tell me that there was another woman floating around here. Why didn't you tell me about Maxine Galbraith?'

'Maxine? I didn't give her a thought—nor need you, I assure you.'

At least Clive had the grace to look embarrassed. Under his tan his face looked more ruddy than ever. Sara gave him an ironic glance.

'No? Isn't possession nine points of the law, and it seems to me that Madame Maxine is very much in possession.'

'Maxine has been company for Drew while all this has been going on. She's out in the wilderness a lot, where unfortunately Drew can't follow her. I don't expect she'll be here for long.'

'And nor will I. Really, Clive, I wouldn't have expected you to bring me on a fool's errand like this. Drew is obviously very involved with Maxine—there was no need for me to come at all. What good do you think I can do?'

'I should think quite a lot when Drew has got over the first shock of meeting you again,' said Clive. 'I thought you and Drew should have a chance before Maxine took over completely.'

'So that's it! You did want to effect a grand reconciliation.'

'Why not?' he persisted. 'I happen to believe that you two were meant for each other, and I don't happen to think that Maxine is good for Drew.'

'So you decided to play God. Really, Clive, it was too bad to drag me all the way here when I could do no good by coming!' said Sara crossly. 'Now you can just arrange for me to go back to Windhoek first thing in the morning.'

'And I thought you were a fighter,' he shrugged.

'What do you mean?'

'I mean I never expected you to give in so easily. Why should you be willing to hand Drew over to Maxine without any fight? Believe me, Sara, Maxine isn't any good for Drew. She's too domineering, too possessive.'

Sara laughed, and the people dining near their table turned around and smiled sympathetically, thinking no doubt that here was a pretty girl enjoying herself with her boy-friend.

'Isn't that what Drew needs? Some domineering, possessive female who'll stand up to him? Goodness knows he was domineering and possessive with me. Now maybe he'll get a taste of his own medicine.'

Clive shook his head.

'I don't like it, Sara. He's in a difficult mood at this time. Don't laugh—he's like Samson when his strength had been taken away. And this woman may just take over. I tell you, Sara, a woman like that could swallow him whole.'

'Oh, Clive, you make her sound like a boa-constrictor!' she teased.

'That's just how she seems to me. Stay here, Sara, please. You can't say Drew wasn't pleased to see you. I watched your meeting, and it didn't look like two people who hated each other.'

'Perhaps it didn't, but you were at a safe distance. You surprise me, Clive,' she added.

'I'm only thinking of your good—you and Drew.'

'Oh, really, Clive, you know how I hated it here before. You know I was completely unsuited to this life. How could I possibly reconcile myself to it now when Drew treats me as an enemy? No, Clive, I can do no good here. My life here, such as it was, is finished. Please arrange for me to go back tomorrow.'

Clive sighed heavily.

'I didn't think you were the kind who ran away from problems, Sara.'

'Didn't you? You've forgotten, I ran away three years ago because I found this life insupportable. I'm three years older now, and wiser, and have made my own life. Drew has no more need of me, nor I of him, even if he does have this problem. I'm not being hardhearted, Clive, but there's nothing I can do for him that Maxine obviously couldn't do better.'

'So you'll just give him over to Maxine without a fight?'

'I finished fighting when I left here,' she said flatly. 'This is a rugged place, Clive, and it breeds rugged people here. Give me the rat-race of Paris any time. I can't take the wilderness.'

Clive's blue eyes were troubled.

'You've become harder, Sara. I thought when you saw Drew like this, you would want to do your utmost to help him.'

'How can I help him when he already has someone who has taken him over,' she sighed. 'I should have known better than to come here. As I told you before, this section of my life was finished three years ago. If you'd hoped to revive it, Clive, you were very much mistaken.'

'Surely, Sara, there must be some feeling left in you for Drew? Did that embrace I saw him give you mean nothing at all?'

'I'm not going to answer that, Clive. I mean it when I say first thing tomorrow I want out from this place.'

Alone in her isolated hut that night, Sara thought over Clive's words. Surely there must be some feeling left in her for Drew? She remembered the terrible pain at her heart when she had first seen him, and then the touch of his hands upon her body, so familiar and yet now so strange. Oh yes, Clive, there had been some kind of feeling, too much in fact. It was Drew who seemed to be without feeling. I can do no good here, she thought; I can only start suffering again. Tomorrow I'll make my way back to the Cape. Before Clive started all this I had my life on an even keel. I must go back and forget this ever happened. What has happened to Drew is a terrible thing, but there's no role in his life that he wants me to play. This Maxine seems to be providing all the female companionship he desires.

The room was not air-conditioned and the small electric fan provided kept up a monotonous, irritating creaking. It was terribly hot. Sara had forgotten just how hot it could be before the rains came. In June and July the days were hot but the nights often cold enough to wear sweaters, but this now was the hottest month before the rains that were eagerly awaited and yet made the roads impassable.

The night was full of strange sounds, strange indeed after the familiar clamour of Paris traffic, the rattle of the taxis, the screaming shout of the klaxons, and yet they were well known to her, for they had become familiar to that young girl who had come with such high hopes to Etosha, the lonely yip of a jackal, the squabbling of monkeys, the bark of a bat-eared fox, some night bird way across the sandy wastes of the plains, and then, silencing all other noises, the commanding roar of a lion. She felt confined and restricted in the little room with its hard mattress and its noisy fan which only emphasised the stifling airlessness around her. I'm not going to sleep, she thought. I must take a walk around the camp to get some air. She knew she would be quite safe because the fences on the perimeter of the camp were very high, too high for any invading animal to penetrate, and at night the gates were securely fastened.

Out of the hut, she was at first overwhelmed by the frightening immensity of the sky. The brilliant stars of the Southern Hemisphere seemed to swing in dizzy arcs over her head and the Milky Way stretched in a great band across the heavens. The lights around the paths were kept on all night and on the other side of the camp she could see the floodlights shining upon the waterhole. Some of the tourists might still be watching. Sara moved towards there, feeling the need for some contact with people.

But there was no one there. No other person, that was. Knee-deep in the pool, an elephant stood motionless like some great piece of rock and a giraffe peered nervously from behind a bush. Sara had forgotten what an impact the sight of an elephant could have, how weird, how astonishing the great beast could be. It was so close, just on the other side of the wall, and yet completely unaware of her presence. The wind must be blowing towards her so that the animal had not detected her scent. She could hear the bubbling sound in its stomach, a sign that it had just taken water. A zebra, more sure of itself than the giraffe, ventured near the water, its thirst impelling it to be brave and face the great bulk of the elephant. It stooped to drink and the bigger animal seemed to tolerate it for a few seconds, but then the huge ears flapped ominously and its head swung threateningly in the zebra's direction. The zebra didn't wait for a second warning but turned tail, its thirst only half appeased. Another elephant appeared as if by magic. Suddenly it was there, another grey bulk coming out of the dark into the illuminated pool. It caressed the other elephant with its trunk like someone greeting an old friend.

'After all those years in Paris, you still use the same perfume.'

Sara swung around at the sound of Drew's voice. He had come here as silently and swiftly as that elephant on the other side of the pool.

'How did you know I was here?' she asked.

'Oh, I'm like one off the cat family since this happened to me. I can see better at night. I can see shapes and forms quite well. The only trouble is that everything is a uniform grey or black, so life appears more hopeful at this time because I'm less at a disadvantage. However, I'd still like to be able to see the red-gold of your hair. Is it still that colour? You haven't changed it in Paris, by any chance?'

'It's still as it was, Drew. I haven't changed its colour or its style—at least, that's not strictly true. Madame insists I change it into all kinds of styles. That's why she prefers me to keep it long.'

'It's as long as it was then?'

'I think so.'

She saw his hand reach out and felt its light touch on

her hair, smoothing the silky strands, brushing them away from her face. And at this light, almost butterfly touch, she felt a deep thrill curve and pulsate somewhere inside her like the first faint flutters of an embryo child. She had a mad impulse to escape, to run away from this terrible re-arousal of the feelings she had once held for this man, but she stood her ground. After all, what had Drew left but his sense of touch? Naturally he was curious as to how she looked if he had not seen her for three years. With his probing nature it was only natural he should want to satisfy this curiosity. His hand fell away from her hair and the fearful throbbing of her heart slowed down.

'Yes,' he said, 'it's just the same, though now to me it looks grey, and yet I can feel through my fingers that wonderful silky sheen. I used to think it was like molton gold.'

'Please, Drew, don't remind me,' she begged.

'Yes, I agree those times are best forgotten. It's all in the past now, Sara, for both of us, isn't it?'

'Of course.'

Of course it was in the past. He had ceased to love her before she even left here, and now there was this other woman, Maxine, strong and beautiful, with the courage to face life in wild places. What could be more suitable? And as for herself, she had made her life far away from here in Paris, a glamorous life that could not be more different from this one here. It was just unfortunate that Drew's touch could still arouse feelings that would be far better forgotten.

Unfortunate, but a warning that she had better heed. She should never have come here. The whole affair had been absurd. This man standing beside her was as rocklike as that elephant, and he could still arouse in her a kind of fear. It's true, she thought, you need courage for this kind of life, and I never had enough. I was brought up to feel safe and spoiled, so how could I get used to living in such a wilderness?

At her side, Drew was as still as an animal that sniffs the air for possible danger. What was he thinking? He had always had this way of keeping silent when most she wanted him to speak. Only in moments of intense emotion did he seem to have the gift of words. That was why this wilderness life suited him, because he was always comfortable with silence, at ease in a wild country.

'Tell me about Paris,' he said now. 'Who is this Madame who rules your life and tells you how to do your hair? Is it good being a model? Is it what you always wanted?'

'Madame? Yes, it's true that I changed one tyrant for another,' she agreed.

'Tyrant? Is that what you thought of me?'

'You were pretty good at telling me how I should lead my life here—but let's not go into that again. As you say, it's all in the past.'

'And if I was overbearing on occasion, it was only for your own safety. You were very young and often too impulsive. Remember that time when you brought that bat-eared fox into the camp and it tore the place apart?'

'I remember,' said Sara. 'But you didn't give me much chance to take an interest in your field work, did you?

'You treated me as an ignorant fool without courage most of the time.'

'And the rest of the time?'

How well she remembered that twisted smile, the expressive curve of the lips that had always held for her some sexual meaning.

'The rest of the time was something else again. I was very young and foolish. It's best forgotten.'

'Young, foolish, passionate, adorable. Where did we go wrong, Sara? No, don't tell me—I know. I was too old for you, and I should never have expected someone like you to like the wilderness. It was too much to ask of a young girl used to the bright lights and to luxury living. But we've gone a long way from Paris. You were going to tell me about your life there.'

'It's—it's—well, it's just life in Paris,' Sara shrugged. 'The work's hard, not as glamorous as it's made out to be. Long hours, lots of time spent standing being fitted. But some of it is fun. There's lots of companionship with the other girls—and jealousy as well, of course. I have a small apartment not far from the Sacré Coeur. It's quite high up, you can see the rooftops.'

'*La vie de bohême*—just what you always wanted,' Drew said wryly. 'And who shares this life?'

'Let's not go into that. It can't mean anything to you any more, can it?'

'No, of course not. Let's just put it down to my natural curiosity. After all, you were my wife. Still are, for that matter.'

'But I was your ex-wife when you introduced me to Maxine,' she reminded him.

'Ah, well, you must admit that the situation is a bit unusual. We haven't seen each other for three years, and yet legally we're still bound together.'

'We don't need to be bound, as you call it. We should have done something about it long ago, that's obvious.'

'I haven't up to now felt any need to change the status quo. However, your arrival came as rather a surprise, and for the last few hours I've been giving it some thought,' Drew told her.

I suppose he's been discussing it with Maxine, Sara thought, and the idea of this woman and Drew talking over their past gave her a pain deep inside herself.

'I've come to the conclusion,' Drew continued, 'that with the way things are we might as well legalise our separation. I expect that's what you want, isn't it?'

The way things are? Did he mean that now he had met Maxine, he intended to marry her?

'Does that mean you intend to marry again?' she asked bluntly.

In the shadowy darkness she saw the ironical glitter of his smile.

'Hardly. Didn't we both come to the conclusion two years ago that I'm just not the marrying kind? Besides, who would have me in my present state?'

'There are handicaps worse than yours,' she retorted.

'You mean I'm feeling too sorry for myself?'

'It seems like that to me.'

Sara knew that Drew would not be able to stand pity and that the only way to treat him was to arouse him out of this well of despondency into which he seemed to have fallen. But it was difficult. She had a stupid, almost overwhelming impulse to take him in her arms, to place her cheek against the rough stubble of his chin, to console and comfort him in the only way she knew how. But that kind of thing was all finished between them long ago.

'Do you realise what my life is like now, Sara?' Drew demanded. 'I'm confined to this place, never allowed to go out because they're all afraid I would do something rash. I might as well be a prisoner in a concentration camp! I can't blame them. They all have different jobs to do and we're short-staffed. You can't expect them to take me around, to risk mishaps that might befall a man who may be going blind, who only sees animals in grey outline. Why, even those two elephants look like cardboard cut-outs to me.'

'What about Maxine?' she asked. 'Can't you go with her?'

'Certainly not! She has to take photographs in all kinds of situations. She has a lot of courage, but I'm not going to be a handicap to anyone. Besides, she has an assistant with her, so there wouldn't be room for me in the party.'

What he means is that he has too much pride to be a hindrance to someone who attracts him strongly, Sara thought. Oh, Drew, you haven't got the humility to find yourself in this position, have you? You just can't stand being dependent on other people. You never would share your life even with me. So what's to become of you?

Suddenly to her own astonishment she heard herself saying, 'I could take you around while I'm here. You could direct me where you wanted to go.'

'You? But you were always scared of the place. You hated going into the wilderness area.'

'You didn't give me much encouragement. You

preferred to leave me alone in the camp. Let's face it, Drew, you always wanted the best of both worlds, to have me there like a kind of doll at the end of the day, but to enjoy the solitude of your real life on your own.'

In the half light she could see the dark glitter of his eyes, and his hands came down on her shoulders now, smoothing the silky skin of her upper arms as he turned her towards him.

'Let's not start this again. You were my wife. It was your idea entirely that I treated you as a doll—I never thought so. But there were and still are terrible hazards to this life. It seemed to me then that you were too young to understand.'

'But I'm not too young now. If it would be of any help to you, I'm willing to go around with you for a few days at least. That's what I came for, to be of some help.'

'I doubt very much whether anyone can be of much help to me now,' said Drew coldly.

'You amaze me! I'm astonished to hear you speak like that, you who were always the most aggressive of men!'

'You really have a very low opinion of me, haven't you, Sara?' he said bitterly.

'It doesn't necessarily mean I have a low opinion just because I say you're aggressive. Some men might even take it as a compliment.'

'Well, let it pass, but if we didn't get on when we lived as husband and wife, how do you think you can bear to be with me on these journeys into the wilderness?'

'I can try. It won't be for ever,' Sara pointed out. 'Even if it works, it can only be for two weeks. I'm due back in Paris very soon. But it might give you a start to making your life over again.'

'But you were frightened of the wilderness even when you were with me and I was—how shall I put it?—a whole man not handicapped by loss of sight.

'How many times did you allow me to accompany you into the wilderness? I never had a chance to get used to it. Believe me, Drew, I've had to face some wild animals in Paris, even if they're of a different kind. I hope I have more courage now. And why should I be scared if all I have to do is drive you around? You can direct me. And we'll be in a vehicle. You don't intend to walk through lion country, do you?'

'No, it's true,' he admitted. 'If I could get around to all the old familiar places without feeling I'm being a burden or a hindrance to anyone who should be doing a more important job, perhaps it would teach me whether I'm capable of carrying on here. Who knows? Some animals depend upon smell and hearing and their sight is not so important to them. Perhaps I can train myself in the same way.'

He could too, Sara thought. If he gets back his will to go on with life, the determination he had before, he could learn to live again.

'Very well,' he said, 'I accept your offer. We'll soon know whether it will work, won't we?'

The grey shadow of the elephant had vanished into the bush and the moon was down. They had been standing shoulder to shoulder as they talked, leaning against the waist-high wall, but suddenly Drew turned, grasped her by the shoulders and buried his face in her hair, then just as suddenly he let her go, so that she stumbled backwards.

'I thought as much,' he said, 'Some fragrances are more memorable than others. Your hair still smells of English primroses, cool and wild and sweet. Go along with you now—I'll see you later to take you up on that offer.'

But Sara still lingered.

'Drew, if I stay, it's on condition that you remember at all times that I'm your ex-wife. Emphasis on the *ex*. Is that understood?'

By the floodlit illumination of the pool, she could see the ironic glitter of his smile.

'You mean you don't want any attacks on your virtue? Well, Sara, we shall see what the days bring. I swear to you that for myself I'll be as safe as . . . as safe as . . . let's say the Tower of Pisa.'

'I wouldn't call that particularly safe,' said Sara.

'Do you want me to take some vow of celibacy before you act as my chauffeur? This much I'll give to you. Nothing will happen during the next few days that you don't want to happen. Does that satisfy you?'

'Certainly,' said Sara. 'Remember, Drew, I'm staying here to try to help you, but anything else can be taken care of, we'll say, by female friends you happen to know here. Is that agreed?'

In the dawn light she saw that slow lazy smile, the smile that had once enchanted her. But that was long ago. All the same, she didn't trust him. She must go to Clive and get him to countermand his arrangements to get her out today. She had a feeling she was going to regret her decision to stay. But it was too late now to draw back.

CHAPTER THREE

SARA had managed to snatch a few hours of sleep, although it had taken long in coming. Drew had said they would make an early start, but not too early this first time. She would have to speak to Clive first; he was going to have a surprise!

Away from the concrete paths, the ground was dry and sandy as she walked towards the staff quarters. It penetrated her clog-like sandals, gritty and uncomfortable in a well-remembered fashion. She had not come equipped for this kind of life. Her elegant navy culottes and blouson top with the striped sailor collar were in the latest fashion, a French idea of an outfit suitable for 'le sport', certainly not the kind of outfit usually seen in a game reserve.

Clive was already round and about, giving orders to the African game guards with the smart khaki uniforms and hats swept up at the side. He looked surprised to see her.

'You're up early. Don't tell me you're so eager to go. I haven't arranged anything yet, I'm afraid. I was going to ask if you could go back on one of the tourists' coaches.'

'No need—I'm staying,' she told him. 'I'm taking Drew around for a few days. He's eager to get out again, so I said I'd drive him.'

Clive looked pleased, yet his first pleasure was followed by a frown.

'That's great news—but, Sara, do you think you can cope? I'd better give you a reliable guard to accompany you. You can't go out alone with Drew in his condition.'

'He isn't going to be pleased if you insist on a guard. Is that really necessary, Clive? Tourists go around on their own here, and we won't get out of the car, I promise. We'll just act like ordinary tourists.'

'Can you imagine Drew acting like an ordinary tourist once he gets out in the reserve again? He'll want to inspect everything, in spite of his handicap. He won't admit how bad his sight is. We've no means of knowing how much he really can see. He says he can still see shapes and forms. The great drawback is that everything is grey instead of coloured, but how that will affect him in the wilderness, one really can't tell.'

'Clive, if you insist on a guard it will destroy the whole object of the operation,' protested Sara. 'He wants to get out there in the wilderness to feel himself again. I promise we won't do anything rash. We can sit near the waterholes and I can describe things to him. That's all that's going to happen, I assure you.'

'All right,' Clive said reluctantly. 'But you do realise it's I who will take the rap if anything goes wrong? You'd better take a gun with you.'

'I wouldn't know how to use it. I'm surprised at you, Clive—such an ardent conservationist recommending a gun!'

'There are times when one comes in useful, if only to fire a shot into the air,' he reminded her.

'Well, I don't want one—they scare me. Why are you making such a fuss, Clive? All I'm going to do is to drive Drew around to places where he wants to go, just like any ordinary tourist in his own car. You can't expect him to stay imprisoned in the camp for ever, and you know how independent he is. He can't stand the idea of taking anyone else away from their normal work.'

'It's true, we are short-staffed at this time. Well, I suppose if Drew's made up his mind, you'll have to go, but take care, Sara. You've been away for three years and have probably forgotten how wild this place is.'

'It has fairly good roads for the tourists. I can't go far wrong,' she said confidently.

'Promise me one thing,' said Clive. 'Don't let Drew get out of the vehicle.'

'How can I promise you that? I haven't got all that much control over Drew, as you know. But I'll do my best.'

'Well, all I can say is I hope this brings you together again. It's what I've always wanted, what I think should happen.'

'I assure you it's certainly not what Drew wants,' said Sara. 'He's only consented to be taken around by me as a last resort, because there's no one else around. If Maxine were available, I'd be on my way back to the Cape right now, I know it. But she's not, and I'm doing my Girl Guide's good deed, but not for long, Clive, only to get Drew going again.'

'If only you could persuade him to go back to the doctors, you would have done another good deed. He's so damned obstinate about that. Do your best with him, Sara.'

'If I couldn't bend him when he was supposed to be in love with me, what hope have I now, Clive? But I'll have a go.'

'Good girl, Sara, and good luck!'

'Why does she need good luck if she's going out with me?' Drew had come up behind them and in the soft sand his footsteps had remained unheard. 'It's I who need the good luck if I'm trusting myself to Sara's tender care. Has your driving improved, Sara?'

'If I can drive in Paris, I can take on the Game Reserve,' Sara replied sharply. Her driving had been another bone of contention in that far-away past. Drew had been too careful of her, reluctant to let her venture far on the untarred, rugged stretches of road in the reserve.

'We don't have the same problems as in Paris,' Drew told her.

'If you're going to start criticising my driving before we have even started, I give up!' snapped Sara.

'Oh, no, you don't. You're committed to being my driver now. I'll merely give directions. Any criticism will be merely coincidental.'

'Any criticism, and you can get out and walk!'

'Through lion country? Oh, no, you wouldn't do that to me.'

'Don't be too sure,' Sara told him.

Clive looked startled at this interchange, and yet she was trying to keep her relation with Drew on a light level. If she began to think how different his situation was now from how it had been when she had known him before, she would get too emotional. When she had first seen him by the waterhole, looking lost and isolated, she had felt torn apart. Only by assuming some kind of hard outer shell could she face the next few days.

'Do you feel capable of driving this car?' Drew asked her. He had directed her to the shed where the vehicles were kept. 'Naturally I have to use my own vehicle. I can't use the Park's property for my own personal jaunts around the place.'

It was a smart blue Chevrolet hatchback model, rather bigger than the cars to which Sara had become accustomed. In Paris she had a small Renault 5, very adequate for dealing with traffic and parking problems. She would never admit, however, that she had any doubts about handling this larger car. At least I won't have to face traffic snarl-ups, she thought, whatever else happens.

'Of course I'm capable,' she said now. 'But you'll have to direct me where to go. I've forgotten the routes, if I ever knew them.'

'Don't worry about that,' Drew assured her. 'Most of the roads skirt the pan. I'll know by the different smells of the vegetation just where we are. You can say when we come to any crossroads or forks just to make sure I don't miss them, but I can see the landscape in a hazy kind of way. It's like looking through mist. When we get out into the open I'll probably find my direction much better than anyone thinks I can.'

His tone said plainly that he was determined to show those who thought he was incapable of carrying on in the wilderness just how competent he really was, and she had a horrible qualm of doubt, a fear that he was going to be dreadfully disappointed when he actually did face up to this fierce bright land again. It was all very well to go around as a tourist would, driving on the wide well marked routes, having the thrill of seeing wild animals but with a safe refuge of a rest camp at the end of it. But his had been a different life, not concerned with the tourist trade, but rather with the welfare of the animals both large and small, from the tiny Damara dik-dik, the terrier-sized antelope, smallest in the world, to the elephant, an emperor among beasts.

And now he could hardly see them, or rather only see them as grey ghosts. What could his life be here in these circumstances? It would be better for him to find some other career, but what kind of work was he fitted to do when he had spent the greater part of his life in the wilderness? Would he ever have the patience to be trained to the things that a blind person could do? She could not imagine him in any kind of sedentary job.

'Well, are you ready to go?' demanded Drew.

'Of course.'

She slipped into the driver's seat and he got in beside her. After some initial hesitation over gears, she managed to get started and drove slowly towards the gate and out into the dusty open road beyond the camp.

It was October, the time people in this part called 'the suicide month', a time of increasing heat and drought before the hoped-for relief of the summer rains arrived. Sometimes they didn't arrive. There were parts of this country that had not seen proper rains for up to seven years. It had been at this time of year that Drew and Sara had finally parted, a time when everyone seemed stretched by the tension of living through such drought. She remembered it well—the parched grasses, the tinder dry thorn trees, the earth cracking open where it had been baked by the merciless sun. As they drove out into the road, a cloud of dust arose behind the vehicle, but the car was air-conditioned and they were enclosed against the heat in a small cube of coolness.

'Where do you want to go first?' asked Sara.

'Oh, I don't know. Just drive. It's good to be out again—you don't know how good. Tell me, Sara, would you mind dreadfully if we switched off the air-conditioning and opened the windows a little? That way I'll be able to smell the place. This way I might as well be driving in a refrigerator.'

Sara knew how it would be once she had quelled the cool breezes in the car, and it was worse than she had thought. She was used to the sparkling frosty air of a city. I guess if you set Drew down in Paris, he'd be stifled by the fumes of the traffic, she thought, but here, I'm half suffocated by the heat and dust. She glanced at Drew. He seemed completely undisturbed by the change in the climatic conditions of the car. Indeed he seemed to be revelling in it, taking deep breaths and obviously enchanted with his new freedom and present surroundings.

'Ah, that's better. Now I can imagine I'm really in the wilderness, even if I am only on the usual tourist track.'

But the tourists stay in their air-conditioned coach, she thought rebelliously. And then she thought, it's all he has now, the feel of his beloved wilderness through scent and sound. I'll have to endure it however he wants it. After all, it's only for a few days.

Although it was fairly early, already the countryside was shimmering in the heat of the sun. Over the arid land, zebra and wildebeest were moving in nose-to-tail columns going and coming to the waterholes.

'Stop for a while, Sara, now we're away from the camp,' instructed Drew. 'I want to breathe air that's unpolluted by the tourists.'

'Isn't it rather arrogant to be so despising of tourists?' she asked. 'After all, they do pay for the pleasure of being here. They probably contribute to your salary, don't you think?'

His sunglasses were extremely dark, and she missed the expressiveness of his eyes as he turned towards her, but his chin still had that arrogant tilt she remembered from long ago.

'I'd prefer not to have to think of that. If I had my way, nobody would come here except people truly dedicated to wild life, not the ones who come here just for the thrill of counting how many lions they can notch up in their travels or how many elephants they can scare off the roads. But let's forget about them. Tell me what you can see.'

Sara drew in her breath. She wanted to say that all she saw was a hostile wasteland, dry as long-dead bones, scarred by the constant heat of a merciless sun, but she knew it would not appear like this to Drew. Upon the desolate plain fairly close to the road was a group of springbok. As their vehicle approached the small golden antelope were disturbed and leaped away, jumping high into the air, their slim legs rigid, their backs arched.

'There are some springbok pronking,' Sara told Drew.

'Show me the direction,' he commanded.

Hesitantly she put her hands on his face and turned it towards the beautiful little animals.

'Ah, yes, now I see them, grey shadows dancing in front of my eyes. The same thing has happened to their pelts as has happened to your hair, Sara—all the gold has gone. But I can still appreciate those fantastic leaps. You see, it isn't as bad as it might be.'

Bad enough, thought Sara. In her mind she could still feel the rough male chin beneath her hands as she had turned his face towards the springboks. It doesn't seem to disturb him if I touch him, she thought, not in the same way that it disturbs me. Have sense, Sara. He was your first lover. Of course somewhere, in spite of eveything that has happened, there must be a little feeling left. You can't shut the door on memories like that, even if it appears he can.

'There's a group of gemsbok going to water,' she said hastily.

'Now those I should be able to spot, with their distinctive long horns and their grey and black coats. And those masks of faces. Surely I can see those?'

Drew seemed to be talking to himself almost.

'They're coming up on the springbok,' she said, not risking again that devastating contact.

'Oh, yes, I see their bulky shapes and the outline of those magnificent horns. Did I ever tell you, Sara, that the female has horns longer than the male? But those clowns' faces aren't very distinct to me.'

He sounded disappointed and she sought for something in the wide space of the plain to distract him. Suddenly she drew in her breath.

'What is it?' he echoed.

'A lion—male. A long way away, but walking this way.'

She had forgotten what it was like, the heart-stopping moment of seeing a lion. It came out of the hazy distance, padding purposefully towards the long lines of zebra and wildebeest making their way to water. Where the low rays of the sun shone on it, its tawny mane seemed to blaze around its huge head, making a halo of flames.

'Use the binoculars and tell me about it,' ordered Drew.

Sara put the glasses to her eyes, her hands shaking a little. With their magnification, the huge beast appeared to be only a few feet away.

'It's enormous!' she said, her voice high with excitement and some alarm.

'Stop squeaking, girl, and describe it. You've seen lions before.'

'Not for a long time. They don't breed in Paris.'

Drew wound down the window still more.

'Good. I can smell it now, so that means it's downwind and it can't smell us.'

Sara would hardly have noticed it if Drew had not said so, but now she was conscious of the wild acrid scent of the huge animal.

'Well, go on, tell me about it,' he said impatiently.

'It's padding slowly towards the waterhole. The wildebeest haven't noticed it yet. Its mane looks almost red in the light of the sun, and I can see its muscles rolling under its skin as it walks. It looks so strong. The wildebeest aren't taking any notice of it. I wonder why?'

'It probably isn't hunting, just coming for a drink. I guess it fed during the night. They mostly hunt at night and usually it's the lionesses who do most of the work of tracking. Lions are lazy creatures, very dependent on their females for making their lives easy. They have them organised.'

'It's getting closer. Perhaps you could see it now if you used the glasses.'

'I can see its grey shape on the plain, a little darker than the ground,' Drew told her.

Is that all? thought Sara. The landscape was full of golden light now that the sun had risen higher. The sandy soil, the lion-coloured grass, the lion itself were all bathed in a tawny luminous shimmer hurting to the eyes. And yet Drew saw only grey shadows. The long column of wildebeest and those who had already reached the small pool had become aware of the presence of the lion and moved uneasily, and there were high-pitched calls from mothers to their young temporarily separated at the drinking place. Then suddenly the whole herd wheeled around and with deep grunts stampeded madly, kicking up their heels in disorganised flight, their odd topheavy heads tossed in panic. The lion seemed magnificently unaware of the sensation he was causing. He strolled lazily towards the pool, while the wildebeest and a few zebra and springbok retreated to a safe distance.

'It's true,' said Sara. 'As you said, he has just come for a drink. He's not taking any notice of the animals around him.'

'I can hear him better than I can see him,' said Drew.

The sound of the lion's tongue lapping water came clearly over the few yards of dry still air that separated the pool from the car, and Sara saw with a shivering thrill that his great golden-green eyes seemed fixed upon them.

'He seems to be looking our way,' she said nervously.

'Don't panic,' soothed Drew. 'They very seldom realise that people inhabit cars. However, there are no hard and fast rules for dealing with lions. They have been known to bite holes in the mudguards or indeed have a go at the tyres.'

'That's a cheering thought!'

'They tend to react more if they see a person on foot or on horseback. I don't know whether you remember that Etosha lions have a reputation for being rather keen man-eaters. No, maybe I didn't want to alarm you, but you're a big girl now, and anyway that reputation is probably totally undeserved,

'Now you tell me!' Sara protested.

'There's nothing to worry about. There haven't been any known incidents since 1950, and that was an isolated instance, though grim enough. Some five Ovambo Africans camped under a tree and during the night were attacked by a pride of lions. Only one man escaped, and he had to spend the night in a tree listening to the lions chewing up his companions. That story has gone down in folklore. That's why our lions have such a bad reputation.'

'Well, thank you very much for telling me such a ghastly story!' shuddered Sara. 'It all adds to the thrill of being here, doesn't it?'

'No cause for alarm. It was a very isolated incident.'

'Bad luck for the Ovambos, though.'

'Certainly, but it's a long time ago. There has been time for other generations of lions since then, more used to tourists, better trained.'

How well Sara remembered the teasing expression of his mobile mouth. It gave her a small pain somewhere in the region of her heart.

'You don't need to try to alarm me,' she said. 'This place has always scared me stiff. You should know that.'

'But why, Sara? I could never understand it. To me it's one of the wonders of the world. The only thing I regret is not having been one of those travellers who saw it in its completely natural state—vast herds of wildebeest, zebra, springbok, as well as giraffe, kudu, rhino and predators like lions and cheetahs.'

'But there are hundreds of animals here now.'

'Certainly, but in the 1850s there was no catering for tourists.'

'So you would have preferred to have travelled on horseback and possibly to have been eaten by lions?'

'I could have coped with them. I've met quite a few on my travels in the wilderness. Those were the incidents about which I kept quiet to you, you may be sure.'

'You left me out of your life,' Sara said sadly.

'You think so? At one time it seemed to me you were quite an important part. However, let's face it, Sara, we were ill-suited. We should never have married in the first place.'

'I guess not,' said Sara.

How can it be so painful to admit that, a fact I've faced for three years? she thought. We failed. So what? Lots of people do fail at marriage these days in far easier circumstances than ours.

'Well, let's not go into that now,' shrugged Drew. 'All over and done with. To tell the truth, I never expected to see you again—there's that word once more. Maybe I never will see you again, Sara. You're like a faded photograph to me now. I can't see the brilliant gold of your hair nor the deep violet of your eyes. Maybe it's just as well.'

His hand came forward and she felt the long bronze fingers slide down the oval of her face. For a moment she was held, her chin in his hand, imprisoned by his touch. And then it was over.

'Your face still has that warm peachlike quality, soft as a newly hatched chick. You may have grown somewhat older, but certainly your skin has remained the same.'

How could she make a fuss over his gentle touch on her face? It was fortunate that he could not see her expression. Oh, why was it that he still had this power over her senses, more than any man she had ever known?

She turned the key and the engine roared as she gave it too much fuel. The lion, its thirst slaked, gave the car a scornful glance and started its long plod back to that horizon that was obscured by clouds of dust. They drove on along the gritty road, a cloud of red dust marking their passage. Sometimes the hazy tawny-coloured plains gave way to patches of acacia woodlands, but there was no green leaf showing and the patches of nibbled grass were colourless as straw. On one side was the Pan itself, dry as bone and stretching away to the horizon with here and there islands of trees growing in the imaginary water.

'It's a lake that died,' said Drew.

'It must have died of thirst.'

'You can put it that way. The Africans call it Land of Dry Water. It all happened millions of years ago when the rivers that made it stopped flowing. Occasionally if we get rain, there are sheets of water, and you can imagine how it was all those years ago. We never had a rainy season while you were here, did we.'

'No,' Sara agreed.

That was part of the trouble, of course, the never-ending drought conditions, the terrible heat that seemed to have no end and that stretched the nerves to screaming pitch.

'We're hoping for rain this year,' he told her. 'Maxine and her camera crew intend to stay until they can photograph the change of seasons and they hope for an influx of birds. That happens when the pools are filled. She's taken some wonderful photographs so far, I'm told. She's very daring in searching for unusual shots. We had to insist on her taking a guard—she's inclined to take very great risks.'

Just the kind of woman you should have married, Sara thought, but she didn't say it aloud.

'Go quietly, Sara, there are often lions in this area. A pride of them have staked out their territory somewhere hereabouts. We're passing a rocky area, aren't we, with some trees? We should see them soon. They'll be resting up after a night's hunting. They usually choose the shade of a tree near here.'

Sara drew the car quietly to a halt.

'I think I can see something, quite close to the road,' said Drew softly. 'Oh, yes, there's a group of lions over there. I can hardly distinguish them because they're so much the colour of the sandy ground and the dry grass.'

He rolled down the window on his side of the car.

'I don't think you should do that,' said Sara. 'They're very near and I think they heard you.'

'They won't be interested in us, you may be sure. Tell me about them. What are they doing?'

'The male lion has rolled over on to his side. He appears to be sleeping. There are three lionesses and—oh, yes, three cubs—oh, now I see another one. They're very sweet. I didn't know cubs had spots.'

'Yes, they remain on belly and lower flanks until the cubs are fully grown.'

'One of the mothers is licking a cub just like a cat. The cub's protesting, growling a bit.'

'I can hear it,' said Drew.

'Yes, they're very close. Don't you think you should wind up that window.'

'No, Sarah, I don't. With the window down I can smell the wilderness, hot red earth and lion smell. I can't see the beasts properly, but I can know about them with another sense. You wouldn't deprive me of that?' He took her hand as if to calm her. 'Don't be nervous—I know what I'm doing. I'm conducting myself like a regular tourist. I haven't even suggested getting out of the car, have I?'

'Not yet, and you certainly aren't going to get out if I have anything to do with it,' she assured him.

'We'll see about that! Anyway, I don't intend to confront this particular pride of lions. I know them of old—they're not especially even-tempered. I won't risk it.'

'That's a relief!'

'You still wear your wedding ring?' asked Drew suddenly.

Her hand was still in his, but now she snatched it away. His long brown hands had felt strangely comforting, but she mustn't think of that.

'Yes, have you any objection?'

'Not at all. I just find it curious that having left me so decisively you should still be wearing my ring.'

'Let's say it affords some protection against wolves, not lions,' she shrugged.

But that's just an excuse, she thought. I've worn it all this time because I couldn't bear to take it off. In spite of all that has passed between this man and myself, in spite of all the bitterness, somehow discarding his ring would have seemed the final break, a betrayal of the vows we made together. But hadn't those vows been betrayed already? They had promised to stay together in sickness and in health until death parted them, but it hadn't worked out that way.

Her eyes were caught by a movement nearby. A little cub had left its play and with the curiosity of a cat was making its way towards the car, its yellow eyes wide and innocent. Its mother, lolling in the shade, was not immediately aware of the cub's disappearance from the group, so that it was only when the little animal was very close to the vehicle that she sprang up and looked around her, making an anxious mewing noise. But the cub took no notice. It was intent on examining the strange large object in front of it. The lioness began to move towards the car, and it was then that Sara noticed that she had difficulty in walking.

'Good heavens,' she exclaimed. 'That lioness is limping! She seems to have something wrong with her foot. Oh, Drew, do wind up the window. She's coming over here after her cub.'

But he leaned out as if straining to get a closer look at the animal. Meanwhile the cub had arrived at the car and was pawing at a piece of rope that happened to be hanging from the side of the vehicle.

'I can see her now, looking like a silhouette in black,' said Drew. 'Yes, she definitely has something wrong, probably a thorn deeply embedded. We'll have to take action about it.'

'So long as she doesn't take action first,' said Sara nervously. She was terrified of the whole situation. 'I really think we should be going, Drew.'

'No, wait a bit. I must find out what's worrying her. I may be able to get more of an idea about it if she comes closer.'

'She's coming far too close for comfort,' said Sara.

The little cub was still playing with the rope directly underneath the car, patting it with its paws, teasing and growling with infant snarling. Suddenly the lioness sprang forward, partly hampered by the injured foot. As she landed heavily close to the car, she gave an angry yelp of pain, then seized the cub by the scruff of its neck and shook it. For a moment Sara looked straight into the beast's great golden eyes and expected her to leap at the open window, but the fact that she was carrying the cub impeded her, and with muttering growls she limped slowly back to her pride.

'Make a note of where we saw her, Sara,' said Drew. 'We'll have to do something about that limp pretty quickly or else she's going to be in a bad way.'

'What can be done?' asked Sara. She was shaking and didn't want Drew to realise how frightened she had been in the last few minutes.

'We'll get Clive to come out with a gun to dart her, then when she's tranquillised she can be treated. Otherwise both she and the cub will get left behind and die in a pretty short time. She won't be able to hunt with that foot dragging like that. Not to worry—Clive and I have often dealt with things of this kind.'

But that was before this happened to you, thought Sara. You can't face bad-tempered lions now, although maybe you think you still can. She drove on slowly, still feeling unnerved by this encounter with the lioness. It was not going to be easy driving Drew around the Reserve; he was too familiar with wild animals, and he would not admit that the position had changed now. Sara began to regret that she had rashly offered to drive him. It would have been safer to let him stay in the camp instead of taking on all this responsibility. She glanced sideways and saw that the dark gloom of his former expression had entirely disappeared. When she thought how he had looked when she had first seen him at the waterhole, she could not regret trying to make things easier for him. All the same, he shouldn't take the risks he had been used to taking before.

She stopped beside a pool, a place where a natural

spring arose miraculously in all this arid wilderness. Various animals were clustered around it, a couple of large eland, some zebra and wildebeest. Now she turned towards Drew and he put his hand out and took hers.

'It's good to be out and about, Sara. Thank you for making it possible.'

His eyes were just the same now he had taken off his sunglasses, the greenish-gold of them just as expressive. It was difficult to realise that his sight had diminished to such an extent. When he was trying to please as he was now, his smile could have charmed a marble statue, she thought. Did he know how terrified she had been when the lioness sprang towards the car, and was he trying to make up for it?

'Clive didn't think I could cope with driving you around,' she told him. 'He didn't think I could manage you, and I'm not sure that I can.'

His teeth flashed white against the deep bronze of his skin.

'Clive's a bit of an old woman since this happened to me. He doesn't think me capable of taking any risks whatsoever.'

'I don't think you should either. If I'm going to drive you around, you must promise me, Drew, that you won't do anything rash,' begged Sara.

'As regards you or the animals we might encounter?' She drew her hand away from his.

'As to that, I can look after myself well enough. It's your attitude to the animals that I don't trust. If that lioness had jumped towards the open car window, it could have clawed you.'

'But it didn't, Sara. Give me credit for a knowledge of animals after all these years in the wilderness. I've taken many more risks than trying to see a lamed lioness through the open window of a car.'

'But not as you are now.'

The bright smiling expression vanished from that face that was so near, familiar and yet now that of a stranger.

'Must you remind me of it? Take it from me, Sara,

the thought is with me all the time that I'm not as I was. Why do you think I'm willing to take risks? Because I don't particularly care what happens to me.'

'That's a crazy way to look at things,' she told him sternly.

'Maybe so, but it's how I look at life right now.'

'Promise me that when you are with me you won't take unnecessary risks any more.'

'We might have differing views about that word unnecessary, but very well, I'll try not to scare you any more, at least as regards animals. As to any other way of scaring you, I can promise nothing.'

His arm slid along the back of the seat and she felt his long brown fingers smoothing the bareness of her shoulder. She tried to draw away, but was held fast in a grip that was firm and inescapable. She felt his other hand on her face, then outlining her neck and very gently cupping her breast in a gesture so familiar that in spite of herself tears sprang to her eyes. She tried to turn her head away, but now his hand sought her chin and he found her mouth, touching it first, tracing the outline as if to try to recognise it once again. And then he was kissing her, a slow kiss, soft as a dove's wing to begin with, then gradually growing in intensity demanding a passionate response. But she struggled away from him.

'No, Drew, it's no good. We finished with all that long ago, and I'm not here so that you can make love to me. I'm your ex-wife, remember, and the emphasis is on the ex.'

'As you wish.'

He had gone away from her now and his arms were at his sides. His expression was dark and withdrawn. It's his vanity that's hurt, she told herself. At one time he knew that I found him irresistible. But he can't expect that now.

'Oh, look, there are some ground squirrels in the road,' she said, hoping to distract him from this awkward moment. 'They're running towards the car and standing up.'

'The tourists have spoiled them. They expect to be fed biscuits.'

'They look so charming. Can I give them a biscuit too?'

'I suppose so. They've become beggars since civilisation struck them. Open the car door and they'll be here soon enough.'

'Is it safe?' she queried.

'I should think so. There's no sign of lions here, is there?'

'No—oh, here they come. Will they take the biscuit from my hand?'

'Sure, just give it to them.'

The little creatures with their flat heads, large eyes and bushy tails grabbed the round biscuits from Sara's hand and sat holding them nibbling neatly around the edges. After this Sara drove on and, keeping his word, Drew took no more obvious risks, nor did he try to touch her again. His bad mood seemed to have lightened and he enjoyed her descriptions of the scenes around them.

Driving back in the late afternoon, she felt relieved that the day had passed without any untoward happening on this their first day out together. The sun was low and the country that had been harshly colourless in the daytime heat had taken on a golden haze in which animals trekked in steady plodding columns on their way to water. The humbug stripes of a herd of zebra showed up very distinctly, and Sara thought they looked like so many toys. She brought the car to a sudden halt.

'What is it?' asked Drew.

He had been silent for a long time, and now he stretched as if impatient to be out of the car and more active.

'A crowd of elephants about to cross the road.'

'Where? Ah, yes, I can see some grey forms against the darker grey of the bush. They'll be going for water. Have they any young with them?'

'Yes, two—oh, no, three babies. They're protecting them so closely I couldn't see them at first. I think they're just about to cross the road in front of us. But wait, there's another car, a green and brown Land Rover, some yards away. The elephants will have to cross between us.'

'That will be Maxine and her crew. She should get some good shots from this lot, don't you think? We'd better sit quietly so that we don't get in her way.'

The elephants had reached the road when suddenly there was the raucous sound of a klaxon from the other vehicle.

'Good lord, what's Maxine up to now?' Drew exclaimed.

The huge animals which had been sedately crossing the open space in front of the car exploded in a thundering herd, coming straight towards them. Beyond them Sara caught a glimpse of Maxine standing up in the other vehicle, her camera on a tripod, and then they were surrounded by what seemed high walls of shaking grey skin. The high squeals of the baby elephants were mingled with the angry trumpeting of the big bulls and the alarmed screeches of the females. Strong as Drew's car was, it shook as the herd passed on either side. For an awful few seconds, Sara really thought that it would be overturned. And then they were away, re-forming their scattered numbers some hundreds of yards further on.

'What a fool of a girl she is!' muttered Drew. 'Can you beat it? She'd do anything for a photograph.'

'So it seems,' said Sara coldly. In spite of his calling her a fool, there had been a distinct note of admiration in his voice.

'I thought you didn't approve of tourists disturbing the animals.'

'Not as a rule, but this is different. Maxine is really keen to show the world how wonderful the animal life is here. It didn't do the elephants any harm to have a bit of a shake-up. They've forgotten about it already.'

'But I haven't,' said Sara. 'It will take me quite a while to forget it. I don't go for elephants charging around me. Tell your girl-friend next time she wants to stampede a herd to count me out!'

CHAPTER FOUR

AFTER the heat and dust of the day, the swimming pool in the camp looked very inviting. It was practically deserted because the tourists must be changing for dinner at this time. Clive had said that tonight there was to be a barbecue and a dance for the party of German tourists who were leaving tomorrow. Sara had a very scanty bikini, an affair of tiny black satin bra and pants, edged with broderie anglaise, more suitable for the resorts of the South of France than for this wilderness area. The cool water welcomed her into its depths and for the first time that day she felt soothed and deliciously at ease. She swam effortlessly up and down the green length of the pool, deliberately trying to make her mind blank, not thinking of the present position in which she now found herself. But she was soon interrupted.

Maxine stood at the edge of the pool, a scarlet two-piece costume revealing the strong curves of a perfect body, most beautifully tanned. Her swallow-dive was effortlessly graceful and she surfaced a little way from Sara.

'Oh, Sara, I'd like to talk to you when I've finished my swim,' she called.

Sara went to sit on one of the lounging chairs that were around the pool. The sun had lost its sting but was still hot enough to dry her swimsuit and warm her skin, and she tried to relax, looking up at the sky where birds wheeled effortlessly in the golden air. But with the advent of Maxine her peace had vanished. What did Maxine intend to say to her? Of one thing she was quite certain—this woman, so sure of herself and so much a law unto herself in her pursuit of stunning photographs, would never apologise for placing them in so much danger. It would never occur to her. So what else is new? Sara thought. I'll soon find out, I suppose.

After a while Maxine emerged dripping from the pool and walked with a graceful swing of her hips towards Sara. Flinging herself down in an adjacent lounger, she patted herself dry with a luxurious towel and loosened her hair that had been knotted on top of her head. It fell in sweeping curtains on each side of her lovely face as she turned towards Sara, her huge dark eyes taking in every detail of Sara's appearance.

'Do you really think it wise, Sara, for you and Drew to go around the reserve on your own without even a guard to help you if you ran into trouble?' she drawled.

'It may not be altogether wise,' Sara replied, 'but it's how Drew wants it.'

'With your encouragement, I expect. Sara dear, I know you used to live here, but that's a long time ago and I expect you've forgotten what the wilderness is like. I could have taken Drew on my expeditions, but I felt it wasn't safe for a man in his state, and now you, who have had so little experience of the country and its animals, have decided to encourage him to risk the dangers.'

'He's decided for himself,' retorted Sara. 'Don't you think it's worth a little risk, Maxine? Being inactive is grinding him down. He must try to take up his life again.'

'With you? Is that what you've come here for, Sara?'

The other woman's dark eyes glittered dangerously. She hates me for being here, Sara thought.

'Certainly not. I only intend to stay here for a few more days. My former life with Drew is over, Maxine. I have no claims on him, you may be sure.'

But even as she said this, she wondered whether this was still true. It must be. Otherwise, what was to happen to the life she had so painfully built up while away from him?

'And another thing, Sara—it can't be good for his eyes to drive around in the noonday sun. The glare is bound to be bad for him.'

'I think he'd say if it was. In any case, he wears those special very dark glasses.'

'You're determined to go on with this then, to act as driver to a man who can't see the landscape,' said Maxine. 'It seems ridiculous to me. You'd be far better persuading him to go back to the specialists.'

'Why don't you persuade him, then?' asked Sara.

'I've tried, but he doesn't want to leave while I'm here, and I'm afraid I can't dissuade him from that. He enjoys my company. I expect when I leave he'll come with me.'

'Well then, that's all right,' said Sara flatly. 'But as regards not being able to see the landscape, it seems to me he can see a fair amount. He sees the animals, but not their colours. He gets a good deal of pleasure from being out and about. Surely you wouldn't deny him that?'

'No, but I think it would be better for him to go around with someone more experienced than you.'

'There's no one to be spared. He doesn't want to interfere with your work, and they're short-staffed. He wouldn't consider taking any of the guards from their regular work.'

'No, I suppose not, but they won't be short-staffed for very much longer. They're bound to get someone to replace Drew.'

'He won't like that,' Sara pointed out.

'Oh, I don't know. If he comes with me when I leave, I should think I can keep him amused and occupied. Anyhow, Sara, I think you should reconsider your decision to stay on. I don't think it's doing Drew any good to go around with you. You aren't used to this kind of life. You looked completely terror-struck when those elephants bolted.'

There was a scornful smile on Maxine's lips, and light suddenly dawned with Sara.

'You did that on purpose!' she accused Maxine. 'You saw that our car was there and you startled the herd in order to give me a fright!'

And to make me want to leave, she thought. Yes, that was it. Maxine hated the idea of her taking Drew around and she was prepared to do anything to stop it.

But what a risk! And yet she was an utterly reckless person who was determined to get her own way.

Maxine laughed scornfully.

'What a crazy idea! I got some magnificent photographs, I hope, that's all. It was just unfortunate that you and Drew happened to be there. But if a little thing like elephants on the road startles you so much, don't you think it would be a good idea to go back to Paris before you come to any harm?'

And with that she slipped her feet into her scarlet wedge-heeled sandals and drifted gracefully away, her dark hair swinging in a smooth shining fall on the bronzed nakedness of her back.

And what she says is true in a way, thought Sara, even if I hate to admit it. I'm scared to death of the wilderness, and now I've committed myself to taking Drew around, and it's worse than it ever was because I was scared even when he had all his faculties. I must have been crazy to think I could do it. Add to that the fact that his touch still has an incredible effect on me and what do you get? The plain truth that I should never have come and that the sooner I go the better it will be for all concerned.

And yet, when she was dressing for the evening of entertainment, she was as eager, more eager in fact, than when she was to be taken to some well-known night club in Paris. It seemed a matter of pride that she should put on her prettiest dress and make up her face with extra care. For whose benefit? Drew would see her floating cotton voile dress as grey, whereas it was a delicious creation of shifting rainbow colours, but if she felt beautiful she would be using Maxine's own weapons.

As she shadowed her violet eyes with the colour of spring lilacs and drew a pale cyclamen stick across her lips, she thought of her conversation with Maxine. Obviously the other woman was anxious to get rid of her. In that case she's going to be disappointed, Sara decided. I'll choose my own time to go. I owe it to Drew to help him, however difficult our life together might have been. He used to mean everything to me once. Not any more, of course, but it won't do any harm to drive him around for a few days. I can't give Maxine the satisfaction of thinking she's made me decide to quit. After all, tourists drive around the reserve just as we were doing today. So long as Drew doesn't take any risks, we'll be all right.

There were to eat together this evening. Obviously it was easier for Drew to handle a barbecue than an ordinary meal, as the guests, wanting to feel themselves really in the wilds, dispensed with implements and ate the meat in their fingers. They were seated at trestle tables around a central circle of hardened floor where several people were already dancing to piped music, but the majority were content to sit back and make conversation to the background of the savoury smell of open-air cooking while tasting the light German wine provided or the large draughts of lager for other tastes.

Although it was an open-air barbecue, everyone had dressed well, probably because for the tourists it was the last night of their vacation. Maxine looked especially stunning in a black dress with narrow shoulder-straps and a belt of shining gold. The huge diamond worn on a short heavy gold chain around her neck was her only ornament except for the intricately patterned gold ring she wore on her right hand. Sara noticed that her left hand was bare of rings. Had she never been married, she wondered, or, having dispensed with any husband, had she discarded her rings to resume single status? The men had made a little concession to dressing up by wearing more formal safari suits than the khaki shorts and bush jackets they wore during the day. Sara remembered with a shaking heart how she had used to admire Drew's appearance in this more formal dress. Now she saw how bronzed his face looked against the light cream of his jacket. Clive was there too, his face more ruddy than ever by the lamplight.

The food arrived, cooked by the African guards over the glowing coals. There were steaks of warthog tasting like tender pork, sosaties, meat cut into cubes and marinated in a curry and apricot sauce, then grilled over the coals on sharpened sticks. There was also a kind of savoury dry corn porridge that had to be scooped up with the fingers and eaten with the meat, and to follow there were cinnamon dumplings and pumpkin fritters. Everything was done to make the tourists feel they were experiencing a true African meal like the ones the old pioneers would have cooked on their long travels in wilderness country such as this.

Maxine had placed herself next to Drew and had somehow arranged it that Sara was with Clive at the other end of the table with other members of the staff in between. She was evidently quite determined to keep Drew's attention centred on herself. But Clive was good company at a happy-go-lucky function such as this, and he kept their end of the table laughing with tales of things that had happened to him while camping in the wilderness.

During a lull in the conversation, however, he turned to Sara and said, 'Drew has told me you saw an injured lioness. We'll have to do something about it quite soon, otherwise it will be too late.'

'Yes, she was limping badly, and she has a young cub.'

'Drew is determined to come with us when we go to try to dart the beast,' he told her, 'I'm not terribly much in favour of that, but you know what he's like. It's very hard to say "No" to a man like Drew.'

I'm the one who should know that, thought Sara.

'Would you be willing to come with us when we go?' Clive asked now. 'If Drew knows that you're there maybe it will restrain him from taking any unnecessary risks.'

'I wouldn't be too sure of that,' Sara told him. 'But certainly I'll come if you think it would help. When do you propose to go?'

'Tomorrow. The sooner the better.'

Sara experienced a sinking feeling at his words. She had blithely committed herself to this adventure, but now she realised it would be so soon, she remembered the lioness and those fierce golden eyes so close to hers and that look of hatred, she began to have second thoughts. Too late to back out now, she thought. But with Clive and Drew there what is there to fear? Only a hundredweight of lioness, that's all.

A little while ago she had seen Drew and Maxine dancing together. They looked a very handsome couple, both so tall and dark. It was impossible to tell that Drew was having difficulty with his sight; he seemed to be managing the business of dancing very well. How quickly he seemed to have adapted himself to his handicap, she thought. Physically, that was. His mind had not adapted at all. His proud independent spirit could not accustom itself to relying on anyone else for help or to relinquishing a career that depended so much on good eyesight.

Now Maxine started dancing with one of her photography crew and Drew was alone. She heard his voice with that low husky note she had tried so hard to forget speaking to her across the table.

'Will you risk a dance with me, Sara? I promise not to tread on your toes.'

He walked towards her and she went to meet him and took his hands in hers, and now she was in his arms, moving across the dance floor. There were few people dancing and for once the music was slow. She had forgotten how well they had always suited each other. She seemed to melt into his arms as the notes of a guitar fell like slow cascades of shimmering water around them and she was held so close that she could feel the muscles of his chest ripple beneath the bronze of his skin.

'Warn me if I get too near to anyone,' he said. 'It's very odd dancing in a company of shadows. Only you are real, Sara.'

But if the others were shadows to him they were shadows to her too, she thought. Nothing seemed real except the fact that they were here together as they had been long ago, their bodies moving in perfect harmony, the enchantment of the music weaving a subtle spell around them.

I didn't want to feel like this, she thought, ever again, but it's not real. It's just the spell of the music and the memories that come flooding back just because I'm here. It can't be the same for him. He's been here all the time. He got over his attraction to me three years ago. Our marriage never worked—he said it was a mistake. So why should I feel again this overwhelming excitement? Why should I feel as if my bones could melt at his touch?

Drew's voice broke into her thoughts.

'I think we've had enough of this, Sara, don't you? Let's find ourselves a cooler corner away from the crowd.'

His arm was still around her waist, compelling her to walk with him away from the lights and the music and the chattering of people towards the darkness at the perimeter of the camp. He seemed to be able to find his way like some wild animal who could see in the dark, who was not worried by the lack of light. They stood at last by the high fence of netting that enclosed the whole area of the camp. The sound of the party was distant now, echoes of music sounding more romantic because farther away, distant sounds of laughter, the hum of conversation like the far away murmur of bees in summer flowers. And out there beyond the fence, there was darkness, the blackness of the wilderness night.

'Listen,' said Drew. 'What do you hear?'

At first there was only the warm wind, whistling along the wires of the fence with the sound of silver spoons being dropped into a crystal bowl, and then Sara began to hear other sounds, the mournful distant howl of a jackal, the scarey screech of a hyena. Quite close by there was a high catlike sound, a growling and purring but a hundred times more potent than any domestic feline could produce.

'Cheetah,' said Drew. 'Quite close by. You should have a fellow feeling for them, Sara—they move like models.'

'I remember them. We didn't see them very often, but they were so beautiful.'

She was deeply conscious that here she was once again alone with Drew in the starlit darkness of the African night. His hand was still at her waist and through the thin fabric of her dress it seemed to send a flame pulsing through her skin.

'Like you, Sara, beautiful, elegant, aloof, very different indeed from that young inexperienced girl I married five years ago.'

Is that how I seem to him? thought Sara, surprised. Aloof? I should be thankful I appear that way.

'That very coolness issues a kind of challenge to a man, you must know that. Crazy, isn't it? In spite of our separation, there's still some desperate kind of spark between us that could so easily go up in flames.'

'I haven't felt it,' she said coolly, 'I think you're mistaken, Drew.'

'You do? How about this, then?'

The hand that was around her waist turned her towards him and she was bent like a reed flowing in the wind against the taut masculinity of his hard frame. His mouth came down on hers with a savage insistence, hard and sure, and there was no escaping it. She tried to draw away, feeling a sensation of panic. No, she could not be involved again in this enchantment of the senses, these crazy sensations that would not stand up to the light of day. She had finished with all this long ago. There had been too high a price to pay for this senseless rapture. And yet one part of her was shaken with joy. She felt Drew's hands on her body and her breasts responded and tautened as if with a life of their own.

'Beautiful, desirable Sara! You see you do want me—want me as much as I want you. We still have something working for us. You can't deny it.'

She broke away from him.

'I do deny it. It didn't work for us before; it can't work now. I didn't come here to be the plaything you had before. I had no real part in your life then and I don't want any part in it now. Let's face it, Drew—you said yourself we were never suited to each other, so why try to revive something that we both know died more than three years ago?'

He let her go so abruptly that she almost fell. By the dim reflection of lights from the camp, she could see that his expression was grim, his mouth stretched in a narrow line.

'If that's how you want it, Sara, so be it. I don't aim to seduce you into submission, even if you are my wife. But when you're back in Paris, you may recall this night—and what do you bet me, you are going to remember with regret that you didn't listen to your own desires?

'You flatter yourself, Drew. My life in Paris is everything I could desire. I don't need you any more. I came here to be of help, not to be seduced by that famous charm. In a few days, I'll be leaving. Don't think I'm going to regret any part of it.'

CHAPTER FIVE

THIS time she didn't have to drive. Clive had commandeered a large truck to go in search of the injured lioness. She was sitting between Clive and Drew on the front seat, vividly conscious of Drew's nearness as she leaned away from Clive to let him change gear.

Glancing at him once or twice, she thought he looked aloof and remote, his aquiline profile turned away from her, his eyes hooded as an eagle's. They had parted on bad terms last night, like enemies, but Sara was glad it had been so. If she had followed her own feelings, she would be regretting it this morning—of that she was certain. This man beside her still had the power to set her body tingling, to captivate her senses as no other man had ever done, but it was no use, was it? Their lives had parted three years ago and it was better so. It was a matter of pride with Drew, an experiment to find out whether he could still fascinate her into submission. Well, she was not going to give him that satisfaction. Let him try his charms on Maxine instead!

She was glad today that Clive was with them and that they had this definite task to carry out. She felt that after last night she could not have borne to be alone with Drew, though once having rebuffed him she did not think she would have any further trouble, because his pride was too great, the same pride that had made him insist on accompanying Clive on this mission, even though it certainly did not seem wise for him to do so.

Once the camp was out of sight, they were again in the wilds. The scene was almost prehistoric, Sara thought, as long columns of animals, zebra, wildebeest, springbok, gemsbok, were strung out in their search for water, some approaching waterholes, some leaving. She could hear the wild bark of the zebras, and the mournful bleating of the wildebeest, and every now and again a group of springbok sprang high into the air in a succession of bouncing leaps, their legs held stiffly, their heads cast downwards.

Beyond the sparse grass and the straggling trees was the Etosha Pan itself, a place of sand stretching for miles and miles into the distance and pockmarked by the hooves of animals. From here Sara could have sworn there was water there, and yet that was an illusion, a mirage conjured up by the shimmering heat. My own life here was like one of those mirages, she thought, a place of dreams and yet a desert shot through by moments of almost unbearable romance.

They came to the place where they had seen the lions yesterday. It was a rugged spot, with rocky outcrops of stones and trees with thick branches that looked as if they could never break into leaf.

'It was just about here that we saw her,' said Drew. 'You know that pride of old, Clive. We've met them before.'

'A pretty dangerous lot,' Clive agreed. 'Not to be trifled with. However, I don't see them around.'

'Wait quietly—they might be hiding up behind that outcrop of rock.'

They sat very still, then Clive stirred and quietly indicated where there was a slight movement.

'Yes, they're there all right. It's their favourite place in the shade. Can you see anything now, Drew?'

'I can see well enough.'

Sara did not believe this after her experience of Drew's eyesight yesterday. She wondered whether he was trying to prove to Clive that he could see better than was the case. It was so difficult to tell.

'Give me my glasses, Sara. Yes, I thought so—there's the old man and two lionesses both with cubs. One of them must be our girl. She's looking thin, as you said.'

'Yes, she won't last much longer with the pride if she can't produce the goods. His lordship expects to be supplied with free meals with not much effort on his part.'

'This is going to be more difficult than I thought,'

said Clive. 'We'll have to find some way to separate her from the others.'

'Perhaps we could attract the cub as we did yesterday,' Sara suggested.

'Good idea. But at the moment they all look too sleepy to move.'

'Let's try a little music. That sometimes rouses their curiosity.'

Clive slipped a tape into the deck that was in the truck, and the strains of some folk music wafted over the scene of barren wilderness, sounding odd and discordant to Sara. The male lion lifted a sleepy head, opened one eye and then promptly fell into a doze again, but the two cubs, alert to any form of amusement and probably bored by all this inactivity, pranced away from their hiding place beside one of the lionesses and stood staring at the source of the unaccustomed noise. Then one, bolder than the other, approached nearer and sat like an oversized kitten, its innocent amber eyes concentrating on this new curiosity.

'That's the one we saw yesterday. It belongs to the lame lioness,' said Sara.

'In that case, we'll use it as bait,' said Clive.

He put on a pair of leather gloves, got out of the car and, seizing the small cub, quickly brought it, spitting and mewing with infantile ferocity, to the vehicle. Having handed the gloves to Sara, he then gave her the cub to hold.

'Now, let's see if this works,' he said.

He drove slowly away while the young lion voiced its protests in no uncertain terms. Then he halted, some way distant but not too far from the original place. Sara swung around in her seat to face the way they had come.

'She's coming,' she said. 'Oh, the poor thing! She's really struggling. What a pity you had to drive so far away from them.'

The lioness was coming over the dry sandy ground with its sparse covering of yellow grass. She was limping even worse than when they had seen her yesterday.

'I'll have to be quick about this,' said Clive.

He swung himself from the driver's seat to the back of the truck. He had his gun at the ready, the gun that was equipped with a dart instead of a bullet, a dart that with luck would anaesthetise the lioness so that her injury could be examined. The lioness was approaching the truck, her limp more emphasised than ever, but this did not affect the ferocity of her appearance. Her eyes were huge deep pools of amber-coloured hatred. Her huge feet had their claws extended and the hair on her back stood up in a ruff.

'Hold fast to the cub, Sara. Hold it tight now.'

Sara had the spitting growling cub in her arms. It was struggling so much that she could hardly hold it, and all the time its mother was approaching nearer, roaring fiercely as it heard its offspring's distress signals.

'I can't hold it for long,' gasped Sara to Drew.

'You must try. I may be needed to help Clive.'

'Oh, Drew, don't do anything rash!' she begged.

'We'll see about that. How are you doing, Clive?'

The lioness was very near now. Sara felt sure she intended to spring into the truck, but Clive at that moment shot the dart. She staggered and paused, but then came on. She sprang at the truck and the metal door shook as her claws ripped the sides. For a moment Sara caught a wiff of hot foetid breath and the little cub struggled in her grasp, and then it was over. She looked out of the cab and saw the lioness give a kind of moan and roll over on to her side.

'Good, we've got her,' she heard Clive say. 'Now to work on her.'

'Come along, Sara, let's join Clive.'

Drew stepped down from the cab and stood beside the lioness, and reluctantly Sara followed him, casting anxious glances around her. They were not so very far from the other lions, she knew, but the men did not seem to be worried about this. Does familiarity breed contempt even of lions? she thought. But Drew should not really be here at all.

The lioness looked very peaceful now, but its eyes were wide open.

'Is it really unconscious?' she asked nervously.

She was still holding the cub, who seemed to have quietened now. It even put out a pink tongue like a small jonquil and licked her arm with a rasping sensation. She set it down near to its mother and it sniffed at the unconscious animal, then lay unperturbably near the warmth of its flank.

'We'll have to work quickly,' said Clive. 'Let's have a look at that foot. Ah, yes, I thought so—there's a porcupine quill embedded deeply in the paw. It will take a bit of getting out.'

'I'll hold her,' said Drew.

'Oh, no,' Sara objected. 'You won't be able to see if she's coming out of the drug.'

Drew turned an annoyed stare on her.

'I'm quite capable of handling an unconscious lioness, Sara. Let me make my own decisions. Clive and I have done this hundreds of times, haven't we, Clive?'

'Yes, Drew, we have, but maybe you shouldn't take too active a role this time, old chap. Let Sara hold her foot. You are game, aren't you, Sara?'

'Sara! Don't be crazy, Clive. Sara's terrified of lions at this close range.'

'Not if they're knocked out like this,' said Sara.

Quite truthfully she was terrified. She could feel her limbs trembling as she prepared to help Clive. With its wide open eyes, the lioness looked so very much alive. But Sara steeled herself to do it rather than let Drew take any part in this when he was too handicapped to see if the lion showed signs of returning to consciousness. The little cub was playing around its recumbent mother, and Sara wondered whether its small rather plaintive mews might get through and arouse the sleeping beast.

'How long do you expect it to stay like this?' she asked Clive.

'Not too long—I only gave it a light dose. If you

give too much, you have to leave them too long, and hyenas or vultures might get at them. Hold steady, Sara, we'll soon have it out. Drew, I guess you'd better watch if you can detect any movement back there. Would you be able to see if any of the other lions were coming?'

'It would be far better if I swapped places with Sara,' Drew told him. 'But for once, Clive, you're the boss. However, I'll be able to see movement if anything emerges from behind that rock, but you and Sara had better keep on the alert too. It's quite apparent that neither of you think I'm a great deal of use at present.'

His voice was bitter. It was only when he came up against a situation like this, thought Sara, that it was brought home to him how difficult the loss of sight could be in this place. It had been wrong for him to come at all. Clive should have come out with one of the Africans, because Drew was just being made to feel useless and his pride would be severely hurt.

There was a moaning sigh from the lioness and Sara started nervously.

'All right, girl, take it easy!' Clive was addressing the animal, but it might as well have been her, she thought. 'Almost done!'

The quill came out like an enormous splinter and Sara heaved a sigh of relief, but Clive still had to give the animal a shot of antibiotics to guard against infection. He had realised, of course, that Drew was displeased at not taking part in all this, and now, incautiously perhaps, he said, 'Sara, you take over from Drew and watch for the other lions. Let Drew hold her now—he's stronger than you if she starts to roll around.'

'Get up on the truck, Sara,' Drew told her. 'You can see further from there.'

Was he thinking she would be safer there if the lion came to? she thought. She felt very unhappy that Drew should take over at this stage, but she could not argue with the two experienced men. How could she imply that Drew should not do the task he had done so often before?

'Take the cub. She's getting in the way.'

She took the cub with her bare hands this time and it cuddled up against her as if it needed comfort. As I do too, she thought. Oh, please God, let them be quick. Don't let her revive before they've finished.

She looked down at the road where the two men were dealing with the lioness, watching anxiously as she seemed to twitch as if reviving. Then she looked up again towards the place where the lions had been resting. Was that a movement or was it a swirl of dust? In the shimmering heat it was difficult to see. The glare hurt her eyes as she took off her sunglasses trying to get a better vision. Yes, it was true. What she had feared all along was happening. The male lion was still lying lazily in the shade of the rock, but the other lioness was strolling slowly in this direction.

'Quick,' she called, 'come back to the truck! The other lioness is coming this way!'

'Can't leave her now,' said Clive. 'We've almost done.'

'Bang something, Sara. That may head her off,' ordered Drew.

Sara put down the cub and looked around. There seemed nothing suitable in sight, but quickly she seized a spade that was on the back of the vehicle and banged it against the side of the truck. But the lioness didn't seem to heed it.

'She isn't taking any notice. Do hurry!' she shouted to the men.

'Don't panic, Sara. She won't come too near us.' This was Drew.

'You make me furious!' she screamed. 'Both of you. Leave her and get up on to this truck, for heaven's sake!'

The lioness from a slow start had begun to gain speed.

'She's starting to trot. How much longer is it going to take?'

'All done now. We can get back on to the truck.'

Clive swung himself up and turned around as if to help Drew, but Drew did not see his outstretched hand.

'Take my hand, Drew. She's almost here—there's no time to lose!'

Sara screamed as she saw the lioness increasing her speed to a gallop. In another few seconds she would be upon Drew and he seemed unaware of this, but when Sara screamed he suddenly sensed the danger and came nearer to the truck, but in the confusion he seemed to become disorientated and not be able to find his way to the steps. Before Clive could do anything about it, Sara had jumped down and, putting the cub beside its mother, she seized Drew's hand and pulled him towards the high steps of the vehicle. By what seemed to her a miracle, the running lioness stopped to examine the cub and with the help of Clive's outstretched hand they were able to scramble up on to the truck.

'That was a near thing,' muttered Clive. 'It was my fault—for a moment I'd forgotten about you, Drew.'

'What had you forgotten?'

Sara shook her head at Clive. She didn't want him to tell Drew how near the lioness had been to them. She was trembling violently, a reaction from the way she had propelled herself in front of the lioness. How had she come to do that, she who had thought herself incapable of facing any danger? Drew did not even know what danger there had been.

'That was pretty slick work, Sara,' Clive said now.

'She always did panic easily,' said Drew. 'There was no need to rush me, Sara. I was quite capable of getting back on to the truck myself. I'm hardly a cripple, you know.'

Clive started to say something, but Sara shook her head again. Below the truck the other lioness was quiet, nosing at her unconscious relative and licking the cub who had greeted her with squeaks of delight.

'She'll be all right now,' said Clive. 'This other lioness will look after her and her cub until she recovers. She'll be a little woozy at first, but it will soon wear off.'

They stayed there for a while and the other lioness became so used to the idea of their presence that she came to lie down in the shade of the truck. All trace of human smell was being thoroughly licked away from the little cub, who protested a little at the rough treatment being dealt out by its aunt.

For the moment the danger was past, thought Sara, but there would be other incidents like this just as long as Drew insisted on trying to lead the life he had had before this happened to him. And in a way I've encouraged him to think he can, she mused. But it's obvious he can't any more. How did I find the courage to get him back on to the truck? Thank God anyway that he doesn't know how close a call it was.

The sun was becoming lower as they rode in the truck back to camp, spilling shimmering gold over the barren land. In the shade of the bushes small dik-dik, little antelope only as big as terrier dogs, slipped past, their beautiful dark eyes wide and alert, and giraffe were feeding, nibbling the topmost leaves of the thorn trees.

'We'll soon be back together again after today. What do you think, Clive?'

'I hope so, Drew. There's nothing I'd like better.'

But Sara could see the worried expression on Clive's ruddy face. He doesn't think Drew can handle a ranger's job any more, she thought.

'It'll take time,' he said now. 'Why not stay in the camp and be contented with administrative work, old man? No one knows more about the reserve than you. You could be indispensable if you were willing to take charge in the office.'

'That kind of work is not for me, and you know it, Clive. I have to get back into the wilderness if I'm to get over this handicap. I have to prove that it doesn't mean anything.'

Clive was silent. What could he say? thought Sara. He had seen how helpless Drew had been when the lioness charged, even though Drew himself was unaware of it. He's so darned obstinate, she thought. With all his knowledge, he could still be useful towards conservation in an administrative way. But no, he's always been used to courting danger and he just won't give up. And what use am I to him in all this? None at all. I wish to heaven I'd never become involved again. What good can I do here? At base he was always a loner, even when we were together. He has only one use for women in his life, and I'm not starting that again.

'Hello,' said Clive, as they rode into the camp in a cloud of red dust. 'There's a strange Land Rover in front of Reception. Not visitors, however, because it's an official vehicle. Looks like it's come from another reserve. We weren't expecting anyone. Who can it be?'

As they came nearer, a tall figure glanced up from his conversation with one of the rangers. With a strange sensation in the region of her heart, Sara recognised him. Brad Kavanagh, the man whose unwelcome attentions had led to the final parting between her and Drew. She had thought he was hundreds of miles away. What was he doing here?

CHAPTER SIX

'SARA, by all that's wonderful! You're the last person I expected to see here. And looking as beautiful as ever, isn't she, Drew?'

'Unfortunately not to me.'

The words were like acid dropping from his tongue, thought Sara. All the joy of the day in the wilderness with her and Clive had vanished from his expression. The dark thunder of his mood showed now and there was a look of strain as he cast that black regard towards Brad, as if struggling to see him, the man whom he had always regarded as an enemy.

'Stupid of me,' said Brad lightly. 'For the moment I'd forgotten about what's happened to you, Drew. Bad luck, old man. That's why I'm here, of course.'

'Why?' asked Drew.

'To take over your job, what else?'

'I wasn't aware that I'd given it up.'

'Oh, come on, Drew! You must realise you can't carry on as you are. O.K., it may be only temporary and if your sight improves as we all hope it will, you can go back to wilderness work, but meanwhile the directors want you to take up some kind of work in an advisory capacity. Very thoughtful of them, don't you think? They aren't throwing you out—you've done far too good work for them in the past for them to do that. I've been amazed at what a high opinion they seem to have of you, Drew.'

'Yes, I expect you would find that surprising, Brad.'

Here they go again, thought Sara, squaring up to each other like two angry lions. Only this time it's Drew who's the old lion, the one who's being driven out of the pride.

'Not at all, but all the same, Drew, those high up think it might be a good idea if you took three months' leave and that will give you time to adjust.'

'I have adjusted,' said Drew. 'Clive and Sara will tell you that I'm adjusting all the time. I don't need three months' leave. It's far better if I stay here getting used to wilderness life once more, finding out how far I'm capable of doing the same kind of work still, not sitting on my backside in the office being kind to tourists.'

'There's nothing wrong in that. I've always enjoyed that part of our work. You'll be surrounded by pretty women all panting to have a go at you—or shouldn't I say that in front of Sara?'

'As far as I'm concerned, Sara is quite neutral. Nothing I say or do affects her any more.'

Brad's wicked dark eyes glanced now from one to the other. He's just the same as he always was, thought Sara. I never trusted him. He's far too aware of his own good looks and what he thinks is his power to charm.

'Is that so? Then what are you doing here, Sara?'

What indeed? thought Sara.

'She's come to relax from the stress of her life in Paris and at present she's acting as my unofficial driver,' said Drew.

'I see. Well, we'll have to give that some thought. I don't believe the directors intend that you should go out in the wilderness at all for the present, Drew. It can hardly be safe for you and Sara alone.'

'Who says so?'

'I say so, and don't forget, Drew, that I'm in charge now. And another thing—Clive must have been crazy to consent to your going with him to dart that lioness. Oh, yes, I've heard about that too. Look, Drew, it's for your own sake I say this. While I'm the boss here there are to be no more harebrained expeditions of that kind. Will you give me your word?'

'Certainly not. How am I to get going again if I can't attempt these things that I've been used to doing for the greater part of my life?'

'Then I'll have no alternative but to report you to the directors. I mean it, Drew. I'm only thinking of your own safety.'

'My safety doesn't matter a damn to me now!' said Drew angrily.

He turned around and strode in the direction of his own hut. In his white-hot anger he stumbled against a tree stump that was in his way. Sara wanted to go after him, but Clive held her back.

'Leave him. In that mood he's best left alone. Obviously he doesn't want anyone with him. For God's sake, why did they have to send you, Brad?'

Brad shrugged his shoulders.

'Why not? Because I was the best choice, I guess. Don't look so worried, Sara—he'll get over it. He'll adjust to being partly sighted—lots of people have had to do just that. Now let's talk about something more pleasant. It's great seeing you again. I thought you and Drew had split up.'

'We have,' Sara told him. 'I just happened to be in Johannesburg for a dress show and Clive asked me to come. But I don't seem to have done much good so far.'

'Not to worry. In my opinion you'd do far more good persuading Drew to get some more medical advice than driving him around the reserve. See if you can do that, won't you? Or at least persuade him to take some leave. He's doing no good staying here.'

Of course he's right, Sara thought. And yet she could find it in her heart to hate this man who was so casually taking over Drew's work, the career he had chosen years ago and loved for most of his life. As Clive said, why did it have to be Brad who was sent to replace him?

'This is an unexpected bonus, your being here, Sara,' Brad went on. 'I hope to see a lot of you while you're here.'

'I don't expect to stay here for very much longer, Brad,' she told him.

'I'm surprised you're here at all—I thought you hated it. Still, you always were a sweet thing, and at present Drew seems to need a woman's influence. But you were always far too good for Drew, if you don't mind my saying so.'

'Not too good—just not the right temperament,' Sara corrected.

'But Drew always was an awkward customer. You would have suited most men. How about me, for instance?'

How well she remembered that winning smile, that confident manner. Yes, now she thought of it, she had to admit that her younger self had been a little flattered by the attentions of this man after what she thought of as Drew's severity and neglect. But he had gone too far, trying to make love to her in Drew's absence. Now here he was again, looking at her in that particularly intimate way that could even now make her feel embarrassed and confused. That was his standby with any woman he found attractive. But now I'm better equipped to deal with his type, thought Sara.

'You're not on my list,' she told him.

'Now I'm hurt! Believe me, Sara, I could show you a better time than your French lovers. I always did have a thing about you even when you were very young and naïve, but now you've transformed yourself into a beautiful, sophisticated woman . . . wow, you can invite me around any time!'

'Thanks, I'll remember that,' Sara told him coolly. 'Now, I must take a shower before dinner.'

'I'll see you later, then.'

She could feel his sexy gaze boring into her back view as she walked away. Her swaying model's walk had become second nature to her, but doubtless he would think it was for his benefit. I guess I'd better go soon, she thought now. If I'm not to drive Drew around what good can I do by staying here? Brad had always spelled trouble. She would be better out of it.

There were very few visitors left in the camp now. The main contingent had departed already, but still a few lingered on, reluctant it seemed to leave this fascinating place, even though the heat was becoming hard to bear and more and more the dust devils whirled around the dry landscape. Unlike the previous evening, when there had been several crowded tables, this evening there was only one long trestle table in the dining room, the room that was open to the sky except for the mosquito netting that protected the visitors from all the winged insects that flung themselves against the screens with metallic plops.

Those visitors who were left were eager to talk to the rangers about their experiences in the field and Sara found herself sitting next to a man who, in spite of his command of English, had an accent she recognised as German. Many Germans visited this reserve because in South-West Africa there are still memories of when the country was a colony of the old German Empire. He made pleasant small talk with Sara, having introduced himself as Dr Buchner. She answered him a little distractedly, for she was very conscious that Drew was sitting next to Maxine and that she was engaging all his attention as usual. When they got up to dance to the music of a tape recorder, she could not help it that her eyes followed them, and again that angry feeling arose in her as she saw Maxine's arms wind possessively around Drew as she guided him in the slow romantic tempo of the waltz.

'You're admiring the way your husband copes with this handicap that has arrived with him,' Dr Buchner observed.

'Oh, yes, I suppose so,' Sara agreed, embarrassed.

She was surprised that he seemed to know all about Drew, but of course it must have been common gossip in the camp. A dramatic story, added to, she supposed, by her own arrival on the scene. They were not to know that she and Drew had been parted irrevocably for all this time.

'Although I'm a doctor of medicine, my dear young lady, I'm also a believer in natural remedies. I've been observing your husband and, in spite of his apparent confidence, I think he is deeply unhappy and therefore subject to enormous stress. Now if you were to concentrate on relieving this stress, I believe it might have some good effect on his complaint. Take him away from this place where he meets other men all the time who are capable now of doing the work he knew and loved so well. My dear, if you were to enjoy a second honeymoon, it would do both of you a great deal of good.'

Sara, who was watching Maxine putting her arm intimately around the back of Drew's neck, was inclined to think that if Drew needed a second honeymoon, it was not to be with her; Maxine evidently thought herself sufficient to supply all Drew's needs in that direction. Dr Buchner went on at some length expanding his theme, until at last Sara said, 'Dr Buchner, it's very kind of you to take this interest in Drew, but it isn't like you think. We've lived apart for three years. I only came here because I heard of his mishap and hoped to be of some help.'

'So? What did I say? All the more reason for that second honeymoon, isn't that so? Have some faith in my diagnosis, my dear young lady. I am a great believer in this particular kind of therapy.'

'But I'm not,' said Sara.

'What kind of therapy?' queried Drew's voice.

'I have just been telling your wife that I am a great believer in natural remedies and that you should go somewhere where you can relax, possibly have a kind of second honeymoon.'

Some wry amusement lit up Drew's dark tanned features with a brilliant smile.

'Very good advice, Doctor—the best I've had yet. How about it, Sara?'

'Dr Buchner only said a kind of second honeymoon. It needn't be the real thing. So long as you have some glamorous female in tow, it needn't necessarily be your wife.'

'Thank you for giving me the choice, Sara,' said Drew dryly, 'but I'm sure Dr Buchner takes a much more moral view than you do. You recommend that I should take my wife on this recuperative trip, don't you, Doctor?'

The doctor spread his hands out, shrugging his shoulders.

'It's entirely up to you, sir, but if I had a wife as beautiful as this, I know what I would do.'

'There you are, you see, Sara. When do we start?'

She felt her anger surging up in her. How dared he joke like this when a few moments ago he had been dancing with Maxine, enjoying the feel of that hand wound so sensuously around his neck?

'I'm afraid I haven't time to go with you,' she said coldly, 'I'm sure you can find someone more suitable for such a trip.'

She got up, intending to get away from him, but just at that moment Brad strode over to them.

'Come and dance, Sara. I haven't had a dance with you in years.'

She was glad of the interruption and allowed herself to be swept away across the space where a few couples were dancing to some lively tune. Brad's arm was too firmly around her. She could feel it now, sliding around her bare shoulders and downwards on to her breast as he led her on to the floor.

'How about a smile?' he demanded. 'What's Drew been saying to you to make you look so displeased with life?'

'Oh, he was just being funny,' she answered.

'That's a change, then. He doesn't seem very funny to me. His outlook is pretty grim at the moment.'

'Why shouldn't it be grim?' she flared, her annoyance now turning upon Brad. 'How would you like to be in his position? But you couldn't imagine such a thing, could you?'

Brad gave a short laugh.

'Maybe not, but one thing I know—I wouldn't stay on where I'm no use. I'd get to hell out of it.'

'So that's it. You want him to go. You want to get rid of him.'

'I think it would be a good thing if he went away from here, maybe got some more medical advice instead of struggling to get himself back to form without any hope of being able to do his own work again. Can't you persuade him to face facts, Sara?'

'I don't think I have any influence on him any more, if I ever had,' she said flatly.

'Not to worry. Let's forget about Drew for the moment. Did I remember to tell you how beautiful you're looking this evening?'

Although the other couples on the floor were dancing separately, now he took her in his arms and held her close. She felt crushed, scarcely able to breathe against the hard muscles of his frame under the thin safari shirt. She could see that Maxine was with Drew again, staring in her direction, and she felt sure she must be commenting on their appearance, telling Drew how Brad was behaving.

'You know I've always had this thing about you, Sara—even when you were Drew's innocent little wife, you turned me on. But now even more so. I asked at the office about your sleeping arrangements, and they seem very convenient to me.'

'To me too, Brad. Far enough away from wild animals, including wolves, of which there are only human ones in this reserve.'

'Don't be like that!' Brad said plaintively. 'There's no reason now why we shouldn't get together. Drew and you are all washed up—anyone can see that. And how about Maxine? She seems to be very much the woman in possession. Forget about Drew, Sara. I'm here and I have all my senses—and how!'

'Let's get things straight, Brad,' she retorted. 'I didn't come here to have an affair with anyone, least of all you. I suffered enough once before because of you and Drew's jealousy, unfounded though it was.'

'Ah, but things are different now, lovely Sara. Drew seems to have other interests, and though you may still be his wife, I gather from your sleeping arrangements it's—what the phrase—"in name only". So how about giving me a chance? You won't regret it, I promise you.'

'Your persistence won't pay off in my case, Brad. I've had enough of wilderness men to last me a lifetime.'

'So? And why did you come running back to Drew when you heard of his mishap?'

'Clive persuaded me, but I realise now that it was all a big mistake. I'll make arrangements to go back to civilisation tomorrow.'

'Too bad! I really thought we might have had something going for us. However, no harm in trying.'

Brad seemed to be taking his dismissal philosophically, Sara thought, but what conceit, thinking he could persuade her to sleep with him when they had only just met after all this time. He really was quite intolerable!

She walked back with him to the table and, without wasting any more time on her, he asked Maxine to dance. Sara was left alone with Drew, for the German doctor was in conversation with another guest.

'Did you enjoy your dance with Brad?' asked Drew.

'Certainly. He was always quite a good dancer.'

'And a good womaniser too. It must seem an extra bonus to him that you happen to be here just when he's come to take over my work. He seems to have ideas of taking over my wife as well.'

'Need that surprise you?'

'I suppose not. He always was attracted to you, and you seemed to have something going for him too at one time.'

'You thought so, no one else did,' said Sara coldly. 'But, Drew, why do we have to drag all this up again? And how can you call me your wife when we've been parted for all this time?'

'No, that's right. There's hardly any point, is there?'

His expression was bleak and, against her will, she felt the same wave of compassion she had felt when she had first seen him standing near the waterhole. But what was the use? Maxine had taken over. She herself had hoped to be of some use in driving him around the reserve, but now that Brad had come it didn't seem they were even going to be allowed to do that. So what was the use of staying any longer? However, she would attempt one last thing.

'Now that Brad has come and you'll be able to take some leave, wouldn't it be a good idea to seek some other medical opinion?' she asked.

'I suppose Brad has asked you to sound me on that. It would be to his advantage to get rid of me for a while.'

'Nonsense! We're all only thinking of your own good. Why do you have to be so terribly obstinate about this, Drew?'

'You know me,' he shrugged. 'I can't stand doctors and hospitals, specially when not one of them can decide what has caused my condition. Except Dr Buchner. Now there's a man with an excellent suggestion, a man after my own heart. What do you think of him?'

'I think he's a romantic, and what's more, he knows nothing about our lives. But yes, perhaps it would be a good idea if you took a vacation. I don't think you would have any difficulty in finding some female company, do you?'

'Maybe not. I'll consider it. You won't be in the running, I suppose, to be my partner in this relaxing vacation?'

'Definitely not. Now that I don't seem to be going to be of any use here, I propose to see if I can find a place on the tourist coach that leaves tomorrow. And since I have some packing to do, Drew, I'll say good night.'

'Packing? Does that mean you're leaving us, Sara?'

Maxine had come back, leaning on Brad's arm.

'Yes, I've decided to go tomorrow if I can get a place on the coach,' Sara told him.

'Oh, I'm sure you will. We're all going to miss you, aren't we, Brad?'

'Of course. I'm sorry you're going, Sara. I had hoped to see more of you. Too bad you have to go so soon. Isn't this a rather sudden decision?'

'She wants to get away from us all,' said Drew. 'Once again she's tired of the wilderness. She never could stand it anyway.'

'Oh, why not, Sara? Personally I find it blissful, the whole set-up and all these gorgeous men who run the place. I can sure go a bundle for them. They all have such tremendous courage and daring, don't you think?'

'You're not lacking in courage yourself, Maxine,' said Drew.

That's what he needs, what he's always wanted, thought Sara. A woman he can admire, a woman who can face the wilderness on his own terms. He despised me for being scared of it. Well, that doesn't matter now. Tomorrow I'll be out of it.

But later, as she packed her small suitcase, in her isolated room, she felt unaccountably depressed. Why should she be feeling so low? she asked herself. Was it because she had reopened a chapter of her life that would have been best forgotten? And she had done no good by coming here, had she? Handicapped or not, Drew would always go his own way without regard to anyone else's feelings. It was tragic that his life as a ranger had come to a halt, but it needn't mean that his career was finished. With his knowledge and experience he could still be of enormous help in the work of the reserve. But why did they have to send Brad to supplant him? Just the very last man he would have wanted. That was old history now, but her being here had reminded him of his old enmity. Perhaps when she had gone, he could begin to forget it.

She heard the mournful cry of a jackal quite close by, a lonely unearthly sound in the darkness of the wilderness. Tomorrow she would be free of these sounds that reminded her only too clearly of her previous life here. The thought of her small apartment in Paris glowed in her mind like a haven of security.

Now the packing was finished. She had changed into a short pale blue nightdress with tiny shoestring straps and she had left a safari suit in a fondant pink ready to wear on her journey tomorrow. The coach would be air-conditioned, so she need not fear extreme heat. But here in this room there was no air-conditioner, only a fan on the ceiling that creaked and whirred with a swishing sound as she turned it on, hoping to obscure some of the sounds that came from that wild darkness outside. It made too much noise to have it on all night, but it might cool the room while she went to have a shower. Even the water seemed tepid tonight, but she was glad to let it flow over her in a refreshing stream. She patted herself dry so as not to get heated again, replaced her nightdress and went back towards the room. She had drawn the curtains but left the light on, and now, with a feeling of shock, she noticed a shadow move against the blind. Could it be the effect of the breeze against the screens? But the night was still and there was no wind whirling the sand along the paths. Could some animal have got into the room? It was so isolated, so near the perimeter fence that could possibly be penetrated by something small. But no, she had closed the door before she had gone to the ablution block. Of that she was certain, although now there seemed to be a chink of light as if the door was not properly shut. Telling herself not to be scared, she opened the door very cautiously and quietly—and then breathed a sigh half relieved, half exasperated. Brad was sitting on the bed, and as she came in he sprang to his feet.

'Sara, at last! I thought you'd gone to wait for Drew in his room when I found you weren't here, but I knew Drew was still with Maxine when I left, so I hoped you would come.'

'What are you doing here, Brad?' she demanded crossly.

'Oh, Sara, don't be so naïve! I told you when we danced that I was pleased your room was so conveniently isolated from the rest, didn't I?'

'And I thought that I implied to you pretty clearly that I wasn't in the mood to receive unexpected guests.'

'Surely not that unexpected. Didn't I tell you when we were dancing that I was always hung up on you? Let's face it, Sara, you're going tomorrow, or so you say, and why shouldn't we enjoy your last night together? You seem to have lost out on Drew, but here I am, healthy, and ready to go. Come on, Sara, surely you wouldn't refuse us a bit of fun together? You aren't a child bride any more, you're a big girl now.'

'Yes, Brad, and I'm adult enough to know when I

don't need your idea of fun. Now, please, I'm rather tired. I've had a long day and I'm going to have a long journey tomorrow. I'd be glad if you would go.'

'Don't be in such a hurry, Sara. Just look what I've brought with me. Doesn't that tempt you to let me stay a bit longer?'

From under the small bedside table where he had hidden it, he produced a bottle of champagne in an ice bucket and two glasses.

'How about a farewell drink with me, lovely Sara, and then, if you really want me to go, I'll be on my way.'

Sara gave an exasperated sigh.

'Brad, you really have the most colossal nerve! I'm not prepared to drink champagne with you at this hour of the night. Keep it for someone with whom you can hope to get better results.'

'I remember you always did play hard to get, but I had hoped now you're more mature you would see it my way. Come on, Sara—we're old friends. Surely you aren't going to send me away without even one kiss?'

His dark eyes had a dangerous glint to them as he came nearer and she felt the strength in the arms that seized her in a powerful grip. She was helpless to resist him as he pressed her hurtfully up against the wall, his wandering hands roughly seeking the soft curves of her body, his sensual mouth attempting to force hers open as she tried with all her strength to resist this onslaught. She wondered how long she could keep up this silent struggle as she felt him moving her now towards the bed. She felt the thin strap of her nightdress tear and realised that she was utterly defenceless against the brute strength of this man, and it was no use trying to call for help because no one would hear her.

Neither of them heard the knock at the door, but she felt the weight of Brad's body suddenly lifted away from her and there he was half kneeling on the floor trying to regain his balance. Drew stood over him, his face dark with rage.

'Is history repeating itself?' he demanded. 'Did I interrupt something?'

'Oh, so you already had a date, Sara, a date with your so-called husband. Is that why you've been playing so hard to get?' He turned to Drew. 'I didn't realise you two still shared this room sometimes. I evidently came at the wrong time.'

'You did indeed. Now will you please leave us alone. I came to speak to my wife.'

'Only to speak?' scoffed Brad. 'And anyhow, how did you know I was here? I thought you'd lost your sight.'

'I can see to a certain extent, unfortunately for you, Brad, it seems. But let Sara speak for herself. Must Brad stay or go, Sara? From what I could see of what was going on, it didn't seem as if you were being completely submissive to his demands—or were you truly playing hard to get as he says?'

Sara looked from one to the other. How had she come to get into this difficult situation? The last thing she wanted was to be left alone with Brad, and yet she did not want to appear to take notice of Drew's wishes. Her problem was solved by Brad flinging himself towards the door, but as he reached it, he turned around, his head lowered, looking, she thought, a little like a bull about to charge.

'Big deal,' he said angrily. 'I know when I'm not wanted. But you should teach this wife of yours not to be so provocative, Drew. Good night, Sara. I thought you considered yourself a free agent these days, but it seems I was wrong. Maybe some other time.'

Sara was left staring at Drew. How dared Brad say she had been provocative? Of course he had just said it to annoy Drew. And what was Drew doing here anyway?

His eyes had that golden light that used to indicate some angry emotion.

'How come Brad was here?' he asked.

'I could ask the same about you!' Sara retorted.

'What did he mean by that crack about being provocative? Did he come by invitation?'

'No, Drew, and neither did you?'

'Right, but I didn't come with the same aim in mind.'

'No? Then why did you come?'

His eyes were on her now and she felt very much aware of her state of semi-nudity, the torn shoulder strap, the flimsy nightdress. How much could Drew see? Could he see her now like the grey negative of a photograph, but with bare shoulders and breasts too much exposed?

'Let's sit down, shall we?' he suggested. 'You won't think I'm about to seduce you if I sit on your bed, will you?'

His face had a grey look, and she remembered that the day had been very long and that all kinds of things must have contributed to the expression of strain that had never been there during their former life together.

'No, I won't think that,' she said. I know that Maxine takes first place where that kind of thing is concerned, she thought.

As Drew sat down, his hands touched the bottle of champagne that Brad had left on the table.

'What's all this, then? Wine, if I'm not mistaken, and it's in an ice bucket. Does that mean it's champagne? Brad was going it and no mistake. He certainly meant to make an impression on you.'

'I guess so,' said Sara.

Drew frowned. He was sitting on the narrow bed and she was conscious that he was very near. She was still trembling from the rough encounter with Brad and she felt lightheaded and a little giddy, although she had not even had any of the wine that was sitting on her bedside table, absurd and incongruous in its silver bucket. Drew put his hand out and she felt it warm and strong on her bare knee.

'Calm down, woman! Why are you trembling? You're making the bed shake. I should have thought you would have had experience of wolves in Paris.'

'Not quite so savage,' Sara told him. 'But let's forget Brad, shall we?'

'With pleasure. All the same, I suspect you must have given him the wrong idea somehow. He always did make a great play for you.'

Is he not jealous any more? thought Sara. But why should he be if he doesn't care about me? I was his wife when he suspected me before, but all that's water under the bridge.

'Thank you anyway for interrupting him,' she said. 'But why have you come?'

His mouth twisted in a bitter smile.

'Not for the same reason as Brad, you may be sure. I've been thinking things over and have decided you're right, Sara. I'll seek some more medical opinions—that is, if you'll consent to accompany me to Johannesburg tomorrow. We can drive as far as Windhoek and get the plane there. Once in Johannesburg I can manage on my own. I certainly don't intend to burden you with any more of my company than is necessary.'

'But, Drew, that's wonderful!' she exclaimed. 'Will you be able to see the specialist? Won't you need an appointment?'

'I'll phone when I get there. The doctors said I could arrange things very quickly if I chose to come back.'

'Do you want me to drive the car for you?' she asked.

'On the high road, certainly, but after driving around with you in the reserve, I'd like to have a stab at trying to drive myself as far as the gates.'

'But are you sure you'll be all right?'

'No, but if I find I can't see the road well enough, we'll change over. The landscape is pretty colourless anyway, and I know the roads like the back of my hand.'

'But what will Brad say?'

A smile lit up the face that had hitherto looked so tired and drawn.

'To hell with Brad,' he said.

CHAPTER SEVEN

So at last Drew had seen sense, Sara thought, as she dressed in the pale pink and white striped safari suit with its Bermuda-type pants and short-sleeved jacket with the practical pockets worn over a thin white woven cotton vest. For coolness she arranged her warm gold hair into a knot away from her face, but little strands insisted on curling upon her neck and on her brow. With this outfit she wore long white lacy socks and mulberry-coloured clogs that slipped easily on to her feet.

She was glad to see when she met Drew that he was looking rested and quite cheerful. Perhaps after all the idea of going to see the specialist had brightened his outlook. Maybe he had abandoned that no-hope attitude that had seemed to her so distressing. She hadn't seen Brad again since last night, and she didn't want to. If she could get away without seeing him she would be glad. But Clive was there to see them off.

'I'm sure glad he's going with you,' Clive said now. 'It will do him good to get away from here, specially since Brad has come. See if you can persuade him to take some kind of vacation, Sara, as well as seeing the eye specialist. You haven't used up all your leave yet, have you?'

'Sorry to disappoint you, Clive, but Drew doesn't intend to spend a vacation with me. He has told me that he's only using me for transport purposes. Once we're in Johannesburg, it's goodbye.'

'I don't believe it. You've managed to persuade him to go with you and I don't think you would leave him on his own now.'

'It's what he wants—he said so. Besides, Clive, I have my own life to lead. You don't seem to consider that. If he needs anyone while he's away doubtless Maxine will come running.'

'You disappoint me,' said Clive.

When Drew arrived ready for the journey she thought he was looking much more rested, even cheerful. The prospect of taking some action must have acted like a tonic. And I suppose he'll be glad to see the last of me when we part in Johannesburg, Sara thought. I guess he's tired of having me hanging around. He insisted on taking the wheel in spite of Clive's muttered protests.

'Don't fuss,' he told both of them. 'I may see everything as grey and not in very clear outline, but I realised when I drove around with Sara that, knowing the roads in the Reserve as I do, I could cope with driving here.

'I hope you're right,' said Clive. 'Anyhow, it's not all that far to the gates, and you won't attempt to drive on the open road, I expect.'

'No, of course not. I know my limitations all too well,' said Drew, frowning a little. 'Come along, Sara, are you ready?'

Sara watched Clive placing her suitcase in the wide back of the station wagon.

'You seem to have a lot of packages in here,' she commented. 'Surely you can't expect to take them on the plane?'

'No, it's a few of my belongings that I intend to leave with a friend in Windhoek. They may need my room while I'm away, so I decided to clear it a little.'

So that accounted for the cardboard packing cases in the back of the vehicle. Sara wondered fleetingly whether, with Brad established here, he had some idea that he might not return, at least until he should be cured. But she could not imagine that he would ever leave the reserve altogether.

There was only Clive to wave them off, and they were soon through the gates of the camp and on to the open track in the reserve. Sara hardly spoke, because she thought Drew must concentrate on his driving, but he seemed to manage quite well. In fact she was more nervous than he. It was so difficult to know how much he could actually see, but she felt she must give him a chance to prove he could do this. Certainly she herself would take the wheel when they came out of the reserve and on to the busy highway. Here the visitors had all gone and there was nothing on the roads but the occasional procession of springbok or impala making their way towards water. Drew seemed to be able to see movements, so she hardly had to warn him about the animals in their path.

Was there hope for him, then? With rest would his eyesight come back? Sara remembered what the German doctor had said. It had been ridiculous to suggest a second honeymoon, but certainly he did not look so burdened with stress as he had when she first met him. Maybe this was what he had needed to be pushed into a decision to see a specialist again, and Brad's coming had provided the push, because he did not want to stay and see him take over the work. He preferred to go elsewhere, even if it was to see the doctors he had hitherto scorned.

Already the landscape was dancing in the heat haze, but this time fortunately he had not insisted on the windows being open. The air-conditioning was working and the car was comfortably cool. This was just as well for the road seemed to get rougher as they progressed, and great clouds of dust rose behind them.

'I didn't realise it was such a long distance to the gates,' Sara commented when they had been driving for what seemed to her quite a long time.

'Distances are always deceptive here. You've probably forgotten that.'

There was a glimmer of a smile on Drew's lips. During the years when she had been away, his image had dimmed in her mind, but now with his living presence, she felt again the magnetism of his physical self. Why did he attract her so much when they simply had nothing in common? That dark profile, the brown hands on the wheel, the strong tanned arms and the cleancut chin with the faintly quizzical mouth, the long dark lashes above the gold-green eyes and the quiff of dark chestnut hair over the rugged brow were all meltingly familiar, just as if the long separation had never taken place.

Pull yourself together, Sara, she warned herself. All that's over long ago, by your choice and by his. There's no going back, and you wouldn't want to, would you? We've both gone on to pastures new, so forget the life you had with him. It can never come again. And now you are a different person from that naïve child who was prepared to give him so much adoration.

The road now was a straight line through mopane scrub, small trees with winglike leaves that looked exhausted in the heat of the day.

'This country all looks so alike to me,' Sara commented.

'Does it? There are differences, you know. The route that I'm taking now is different from the way you entered the reserve. Don't you remember that?'

'No, of course not. I haven't got a very brilliant sense of direction. However, I can find my way around in Paris.'

'But not in the wilderness. You don't have to worry though, I know the route,' Drew assured her.

'It seems to be taking so long.'

She had just looked at the quartz watch on her wrist with its heavy gold bracelet and had been astonished that they appeared to have been travelling for such a length of time. She had been absorbed in her thoughts and had not noticed before. Could Drew have taken the wrong road in his eagerness to show he could cope with the driving? But the road was straight and there had been no deviations.

'Are you sure we're on the right road? I don't remember that it took so long to reach the gates.'

'Not to worry, I know where I'm going.'

There was still that odd smile on his lips, and she felt a twist of something uneasy stir in her mind.

'Are you certain, Drew, that this is the way to the gate?'

'No, I'm not certain of that. I only know this is the way I intend to go. This is the journey I've planned.'

'What journey, Drew? We're on our way to Windhoek, surely?'

'No, Sara, we are not.'

He drew the car to a halt beside the road and a cloud of dust surrounded them. Then it cleared, and ahead of them in the barren landscape she could see that the look of the country was changing and that, in place of the flat plain, there were huge rocks that in some other age had forced themselves up, looking like huge monoliths around them. They seemed like temples to some primitive gods, and Sara thought this was the wildest country she had ever seen.

'Where are we? Are you lost, Drew?'

'No, I'm not lost. I had every intention of coming here. You all told me I needed a vacation, so now I'm coming to the place I've chosen.'

Sara drew a breath of sheer disbelief.

'Oh, no, you must be mad, Drew! You can't do this! You told me you wanted to go to Windhoek. What about Johannesburg and the specialist?'

'It was all of you who were so intent on persuading me to see the specialist,' he shrugged. 'I prefer Dr Buchner's solution.'

'This is madness, Drew. Where do you think you're heading?'

'I don't think, I know. I've always liked this part of the reserve. It's unknown to the tourist trade, practically unknown to man. The last wilderness, rugged and beautiful, a place where man takes second place to the wilds.'

'You don't mean ... Drew, do you really mean that you intend to stay here? But how can you? And what about me?'

He slid his arm along the back of the seat and she felt his hand on her shoulder turning her towards him. She looked into his eyes that so much resembled those of some untamed animal, dark gold with something flashing and greenish in their depths. His other hand encircled her chin and she felt his long slender fingers that exerted a force that was somewhat hurtful, strong and compelling.

'You, my dear Sara, are one of the most essential ingredients of this expedition,' he drawled. 'In my present state, I could hardly manage without you. You accused me of never taking you on my forays into the wilderness. Well, now you are being proved wrong.'

'Don't be ridiculous. When I said that to you I was harking back to our past history. I didn't mean that I was prepared to go on some crazy adventure with you now.'

'No? But now you have no choice, have you? You came to the reserve with the idea of being of some help to me, and this is how I've decided you can help.'

'But I didn't decide that I wanted to help you this way. I wasn't even asked. This is entirely your idea, and a crazy one at that. What are you going to eat during this wonderful stay in the wilderness?' she added.

'That's all taken care of. I got one of the Africans to help me to pack stores—that's what's in the packages you asked about.'

'And you lied to me, fobbed me off with some story about storing your belongings. Really, Drew you're completely unscrupulous!'

'So you often told me before you left me. That's nothing new.'

'And where do you intend to sleep?'

'That's organised too. I have sleeping bags in the car and of course we could sleep in the back, but I have another idea. There's an old hunting lodge not far from the track. It belonged to an Austrian baron long ago. It's still partly furnished and should satisfy your ideas of romance. We can make ourselves very comfortable there.'

'You may do, but count me out,' retorted Sara. 'I intend to go straight back. I refuse to go on with this mad idea. Even if I have to leave you on your own, I'm going to drive back and get Clive to come and make you see sense. I'm certainly not going to have any part in this.'

'We'll see,' he said enigmatically. 'How I wish now that I could see the blue of your eyes darkened with anger. Do they still go almost black when something annoys you?'

'I don't know, but if that's so they must be black as night now!'

Sara felt his hand smoothing the outline of her face and then his mouth came down to kiss her lids with the sensuous touch of a moth ghosting its way towards some blossoming flower. She shuddered and shook her head as if to rid herself of the strange sensation of those cool lips.

'Don't think you can seduce me now, Drew, as you could do when I was a stupid child. I was young and foolish when we married, filled with ideas of romance of the wilds. I soon found out how wrong I was, didn't I? So don't think I'm prepared to go along with you in this crazy plan.'

'I intend to convince you otherwise,' said Drew, and turned the key of the car.

They drove on, and now the straight uninteresting line of the road through the mopane scrub seemed to change. Certainly the road became no better; in fact it seemed to Sara to become worse. Obviously it was hardly used at all and was a mere track over the rough ground, but now the surrounding country became totally different in a rather terrifying way. Instead of the yellowish grey sand, here there was red earth and in the distance rolling hills and huge outcrops of granite rocks. The rocks were piled and heaped up together as if at one time there had been some gigantic upheaval.

'It looks as if giants had some kind of war, throwing these rocks around,' Sara commented.

'Pretty sensational stuff, isn't it? I thought you'd like it.'

'I didn't say I liked it. It all looks horribly spooky to me,' Sara told him.

They were at a high point now and in the distance the country fell away into woodland with patches of grassland showing yellow, but even there the huge formations of rock showed through like some kind of primitive monuments. As they drove on, Sara could see that in some of the rocks trees had rooted themselves and now grew out of them in weird contorted shapes.

'I've never seen such savage-looking country,' she said, barely able to suppress a shudder.

'Wonderful, isn't it?' said Drew. 'If I could only see it properly instead of in uniform tones of greys and blacks. This is the true Africa, Sara, ancient and rugged with a wild beauty of its own. These rocks have been battered by the elements for millions of years, and they've survived all that, survived wind and weather for centuries. This is the true wilderness, undisturbed by man. You won't get any tourists here, I promise you.'

'I shouldn't think they would want to come,' said Sara.

How could she persuade him to turn around and go back? As soon try to turn the tide when he was in a mood like this. In her present situation, the camp that they had left seemed to Sara a haven of civilisation. She had regretted coming there and yet it would have been easy enough to go. If only she had got on the tourist coach as she had intended and not let herself be persuaded by Drew! Anger swelled up in her again, tightening her throat.

'Why me?' she asked. 'Why didn't you bring Maxine, if you wanted some female to come with you?'

'Because Maxine would have insisted on bringing her whole retinue on the expedition and I would have got no peace. And she's not particularly domesticated either.'

'Now I've heard everything!' Sara exclaimed. 'You've brought me here to cook for you—well, let me tell you this, you can do your own cooking, because I have no intention of staying in this god forsaken place!'

'Not god forsaken,' said Drew. 'No one has ever left it, because man has never lived here. That's why to me it's so enthralling.'

'Not to me, however. Believe me, Drew, as soon as we've arrived at this place where you're going, whether you come with me or not, I intend to turn around and drive right back.'

'Wait until you see it,' he urged. 'I'm quite sure it will charm you.'

'But you won't,' said Sara. 'Anyhow, how can you say no one has ever lived here when there's this place where you intend to stay?'

'Ah, yes, I was forgetting about that, but it was hardly used. It was built many years ago when this country was largely undiscovered, but it was soon abandoned. The Baron held huge hunting parties there, even brought his mistresses, it was rumoured.'

'No wonder it was abandoned,' said Sara. 'No one would want to live in this frightening country unless they had to.'

'Why do you find it frightening? To me it's one of the most beautiful places on earth.'

The day was far advanced and the shadows of the giant rocks becoming longer. Up until now, it had seemed a land totally deserted, but now Sara was startled to see sinister-looking figures sitting upon a rock quite close by, black against the skyline.

'But there's something here!' she cried, suddenly terrified by those grotesque figures looking like gargoyles on the wall of rock.

Drew jammed on his brakes and looked towards where she was pointing—but of course the figures must have appeared dim to him. He must, however, have been able to recognise them from their outline, because he told her scornfully, 'Good heavens, Sara, even I with my present problems can recognise baboons. They're keeping a lookout while the troop hunt for food. There's no need to get hysterical about them.'

'I'm not hysterical, merely startled,' she told him indignantly. 'The landscape here has seemed so dead up until now.'

'Only the usual inactivity in the heat of the sun. There'll be plenty of life around now.'

On the granite boulders, hyrax, a kind of rock rabbit, sat motionless but uttering warning shouts as they saw the moving vehicle and a troop of mountain zebras crossed the road on their evening trek for water. Some

gemsbok with their black and white clown's faces
looked up startled from some sparring play they were
having with each other, their sharp horns clashing.

'Are there lions here?' asked Sara.

'Naturally.'

'That's all I need—a vacation with lions on my
doorstep! Not that I mean to stay, of course.'

'You've made that plain,' Drew said coldly.

Along the road there was a flash of white through the
scrub and suddenly, startlingly, Sara saw the lodge. It
was like something in a fairy tale, white against the
darkness of the landscape, with turreted walls and small
slits for windows.

'Here we are,' said Drew. 'How do you like your
home for the next couple of weeks?'

'It may be yours, but it's certainly not mine,' Sara
told him. 'As soon as you've unpacked your packages, I
intend to go back.'

'A least have a look at the place first,' he urged.

'You don't think that will alter my mind, do you?'

As they approached the building, a blueheaded lizard
that had been sunning itself on the path scuttled away
in front of them.

'Will there be snakes?' asked Sara nervously.

'You never know,' said Drew.

How infuriating this man was! she thought. He was
actually smiling now at her discomfiture. He put an arm
around her and guided her into the lodge. It was
whitewashed inside too and the floors in patterned tiles
were only a little dusty.

'How is it that it's kept so clean?' Sara asked. 'And
who keeps the place whitewashed?'

'Some workers are sent from the camp to clean it up
each spring before the tourist season. Not, of course,
that any visitors come here, but it's an historical
monument and they don't want it to fall into disrepair.'

'The spiders appreciate it,' said Sara, shuddering. She
had just seen a huge web in a corner of the room, with
an enormous malevolent-looking spider which seemed
to be staring straight at them.

'We'll soon rid ourselves of the livestock,' Drew assured her.

'You mean you will, but now I'd like you to unpack the car, because I need to start back the way we have come.'

'I think you've forgotten the fact that we don't have daylight saving here. In an hour's time the sun will set, and you certainly wouldn't want to drive through the reserve in the dark, would you?'

Sara looked rather startled. She had been feeling so angry with him that she had overlooked this vital fact. There was simply no hope of getting back before darkness set in over this savage countryside. It seemed she would have to stay.

'I intend to go first thing in the morning,' she told him.

'That may be, but at the moment we need to make ourselves comfortable for the night. Come and help unpack the car. We'll need the small gas cooker with its cylinder and the packs of food, as well as the sleeping bags and blow-up mattress.'

'You have thought of everything, haven't you?' sighed Sara.

'I should think so,' said Drew.

She would have liked to hit the complacent smile from his sunbrowned face, but it would do no good to sit and sulk while he struggled with the packages from the vehicle, would it? Already the animals of the night were awakening, it seemed, from their afternoon siesta. Distantly she heard the mournful howl of a jackal and the squeals of fighting baboons. What else was out there in the gloom waiting for the blackness of the African night to descend in order to start hunting? There was a noise like that of some large cat, high and agitated.

'Cheetahs,' said Drew. 'Maybe a lion has stolen their kill. They sometimes do. They're all for an easy way to get food.'

'I hope they don't think we're an easy target,' said Sara uneasily.

'Not to worry. We have four walls to protect us and what's more, Sara, I've brought a gun just in case we have trouble.'

'I suppose I should be grateful for that. I never remember hearing that you carried a gun before,' she added.

'It's merely a safety precaution. You know I would never shoot any animal unless I absolutely had to.'

But how can he possibly use a gun with accuracy? she thought. Let's hope he doesn't have to try!

The rooms on the ground floor were sparsely furnished but gave some indication of a past magnificence. There was a main one, large and with lofty ceilings, the floors tiled in intricate patterns giving almost the impression of an oriental carpet, and there was a huge stone fireplace with a coat of arms in the central panel.

'Surely they can never have needed a fireplace of that size,' Sara commented.

'It can be cold during the winter nights here, but I should think it was mostly for show,' said Drew. 'Who knows, maybe they roasted their bag from the hunt over it.'

'It looks big enough to roast an ox.'

There were a couple of old leather chairs there, and a carved chest that was soft to the touch.

'Termite,' commented Drew. 'If it should be handled too roughly I dare say the whole thing would fall to pieces.'

There was a kitchen with flagged floors and a stone sink, and this led out on to a kind of patio. A strange animal smell pervaded the place. Instantly Drew was on the alert.

'What is it?' asked Sara fearfully.

'Not to worry. There might have been lions in the vicinity lately. It's a very strong smell, as you know, and it's inclined to linger. But they must have moved on by now.'

'I hope so,' said Sara.

'Don't panic. There are bound to be animals of some

kind wandering around outside, but we'll be quite
secure here. You can see these doors were built to last.
Let's inspect the other floor, shall we?'

A flight of stone steps led up to the floor above. Here
along a passage there were rooms that must have been
used by the Baron's companions, hardly furnished
except for several old truckle beds, but when they came
to the end of the passage, Sara had a surprise. The
heavy door was made of wood and decorated with
studs of metal. A large knob in the shape of a lion's
head lifted the latch and inside was a room which was
almost circular in shape being part of one of the towers.
It gave an immediate impression of faded splendour.

'This obviously belonged to the Baron himself,' said
Drew.

Dominating the room was a large fourposter bed, its
pillars and head intricately carved with fat cupids and
naked nymphs. The velvet draperies seemed totally
unsuitable for this climate and were shredded by moth
and age. The exquisitely embroidered lace counterpane
was yellow with age and the gilt candelabrum in the
centre of the room was festooned with spiders' webs.

'How do you fancy sleeping here?' asked Drew.

Sara shuddered. 'I'd prefer the sleeping bag and the
blow-up mattress.'

'I thought it might appeal to your sense of romance. I
remember this bed of old. I should think its history
might give you exciting dreams.'

'I don't need them,' Sara told him.

'What I really need is to be far away from here,
winging my way back to some kind of civilisation. Do
you really think, Drew, that this god forsaken place can
do anything for you at all?'

'Certainly. Here there'll be no one to try to order my
life. I can relax here and find out how much I can cope
with the true wilderness.'

'And me?' queried Sara. 'What is my part in all this?'

There was something in his expression that stirred a
kind of fear deep inside her.

'Didn't you come here with the express intention of

helping me? Well, now's your chance. The good doctor suggested a second honeymoon, but a honeymoon implies a continuation of marriage, and that neither of us wants, do we? Let's say, however, that a short affair might benefit both of us.'

'Now I know you're really mad, Drew,' said Sara crossly. 'I haven't the slightest intention of having a short affair with you. I hate the very idea!'

'Are you sure? Don't deceive yourself, Sara. Your body responds to mine even if you would like to think it doesn't. Why do you tremble when I put my hand on you like this?'

One arm was around her back holding her firmly so that she could not get away and the other, with those long strong fingers she remembered so well, had slipped beneath the open neck of the pink jacket, beneath the strip of lace that was her bra, and was cupping her breast, caressing the rosy tip into unwilling response. His mouth came down upon hers, hard and firm, coaxing her lips until they parted, submitting themselves to his will.

Suddenly he released her so that she almost fell.

'I think I've proved my point, don't you?'

Sara hated that triumphant expression, hated herself for submitting so easily to his caresses.

'I wouldn't say you have. No, Drew, there's too long a gap of years for us to bridge it ever again. Let's say that for the moment I forgot who it was who was kissing me.'

His frown was dark and his hands, as they grasped her shoulders, made her flinch.

'So. You mean to imply that you can close your eyes and imagine some other lover as I kiss you. Well, let me tell you, Sara, two can play at that game.'

'I expect they can,' said Sara, 'but I'm not prepared to act as a substitute for Maxine, of that you can be sure.'

'Nor I for some shadow of a Frenchman, so now we know where we stand.'

'Yes, we do, don't we? So let's get on with more practical issues. What are we going to eat?'

There were logs in the great fireplace and Drew put a match to the fire as the night had turned cool. There was no glass in the slits of windows, only a covering of gauze that had been placed there at one time to prevent insects entering, but they were in poor repair, and when the lamp was lit, moths and other flying creatures fluttered in.

'We'll manage with firelight,' said Drew, extinguishing the glow that had attracted them. The light of the flames flickered and danced over the white walls as Sara set about unpacking the food.

'But first some wine,' Drew said. 'I've had it in a kind of cool box, so it should be just right.'

'You certainly did think of everything,' agreed Sara. 'Asparagus, cold chicken, tinned raspberries and cream—what a feast!'

'Better than that eternal barbecued warthog,' said Drew. 'However, we'll probably be glad of some game when we've been here a while.'

Sara let that pass. She had no intention of staying beyond the next day. She was determined that as soon as it was light she would be on her way. Even if she had to leave Drew on his own, it would be better to do this and enlist Clive's aid in getting him back rather than stay in this dangerous place just because Drew was obsessed with this idea of living in the wilderness. Certainly he could not stay alone for very long here, and she had no intention of remaining with him. Remembering her reaction to his kiss, she felt glad that she had lied to him, making him believe she had been thinking of another lover. No other man in her life had ever made her feel as Drew had, but this she must conceal. His lovemaking was a kind of test of his vanity; he wanted to believe that he could still make her react in the same way that she had responded to him when she was a young and foolish bride, but that was in the past.

And yet here she felt a kind of peace, sitting on the low cushions enclosed by firelight. A white moth ghosted down to sit on the rim of her glass. It put out a long proboscis and sipped curiously at her wine. A cricket set up a cheerful chirruping somewhere near the fireplace.

They had dragged a mattress in front of the fireplace and now Drew brought his wine and came to sit beside her. By this light his features looked clearcut as if hewn from stone. In Paris Sara had become used to sophisticated city men who would have been totally bewildered by this setting, but here Drew was naturally at home. She tried to remember the men who escorted her in Paris, took her to theatres, dined her at exclusive restaurants, but this man sitting beside her came between her and them, so that they seemed like puppets with their sleek hairdos and suave manners. Only Drew seemed real.

Beyond the firelit room in the black night of the wilderness, the sounds seemed to Sara menacing and sinister. Insects sang and sighed and shrieked as if they were human, and again there was a high-pitched scream as if something were in torment.

'No wonder people believe in witches!' she shuddered.

'Not to worry—I can explain every sound to you. That squeal is probably merely a baboon which has gone to sleep too near the edge of a slope and fallen off, or maybe a leopard has got it. Baboons are their favourite food.'

Suddenly, quite near it seemed to Sara, there was the roar of a lion, threatening every other wild creature out there in the wilderness. It seemed to echo across the savage land, filling the night with menace. Drew was smiling now, his expression rapt and fascinated.

'Did you ever hear anything more magnificent?' he asked Sara.

'It sounds terrifying to me!'

'No need. They usually roar after they've killed, not before. What you hear is the sound of a satisfied beast. However, the lioness usually does the hunting for him. Very well trained, are lionesses.'

'It sounds like it,' said Sara.

She was all too conscious now of his nearness, the lithe strength of his body, the warmth of his thigh next to hers. As they ate the quite luxurious supper he had provided from tins, the tension she had felt over the whole situation began to vanish, but she told herself she must remain on her guard. She could so easily let herself be persuaded and it would be unutterably foolish to let Drew have his way. A short affair? No, she did not want any more unhappy memories to take back to Paris. And in the end it would be unhappy. A love affair with this man who was her husband now only in name could bring her nothing but grief.

'That was good,' he said, stretching himself like a lazy, satisfied cat. 'Talking of lions, did you know, Sara, that it's usually the female who initiates the lovemaking? She's so very keen that the lion has his work cut out to keep her satisfied. What do you think of that for animal passion?'

'I think I would prefer not to be a lioness,' said Sara primly. 'And now I must wash up. How is it, Drew, that there's a water supply here?'

'It comes from a spring, and there's even a septic tank here. All mod cons, in fact. Now, Sara, why did you change the subject from lovemaking to such mundane chat? The plates are disposable anyway. As you said before, I think of everything. Strange as it may seem, I didn't bring you here to do the washing up. I brought you here to be my eyes, but I also brought you here to make love to you.'

The flames had died down and the room was not as light, but in the golden glow of the embers Drew's face looked dark and alive with that smile that had so often charmed her in the past. How easy it would be to fall in with his wishes! She was filled with a kind of tremulous ecstasy and every cell in her body seemed to long for his touch. Desire seized her as it had when she was just a girl responsive to his every wish, and she felt the same kind of suffocating excitement as she had in those far-off days lying under the intimate shelter of the net draped over their marriage bed.

But now she knew that those nights of ecstasy had
led to nothing but heartbreak, and so they could again,
if she were so foolish as to yield to him. Their paths of
life had led too far away from each other, on too
diverse ways, and there could be no going back. She
hated his way of life and, if it were ever put to him, he
would loathe hers. Imagine Drew in a city! She could
not help smiling at the thought.

'Does the thought of my making love to you make
you smile? I wonder, is that a good sign or a bad?'
queried Drew.

She was surprised that he had been able to detect it,
and yet his face was so close to hers now and he had
said he could see better in the dark. His hands were on
her face smoothing the lines of her cheekbones as if he
sought to read her expression. Then one hand was at
her nape feeling the sensitive area behind the weight of
her hair.

'How is it you have hair made of softest silk?' he
asked. 'I can only imagine the colour, spun gold in the
light of the fire. You belonged to me once, Sara, and
now I intend you should belong to me again.'

His arms were on her shoulders now, pressing her
down upon the mattress, and she felt his hand sliding
beneath her thin jacket, easily releasing the clasp of her
bra. His kisses had a savage insistence she had never
known before and she felt the steel-like hardness of his
body pressing down upon her, willing her with no
words into submission to this desperate enchantment of
the senses. With a supreme effort of will she thrust
herself away from him.

'Won't you be convinced, Drew, that I want no part
in this? If you'd wanted an affair, you should have
brought Maxine. I'm not prepared to give you the kind
of therapy that Dr Buchner recommends. I didn't come
here to Etosha for that. On my part that was all over
long ago.'

He drew away from her and his frown was dark, but
he shrugged his shoulders and smiled with little
suggestion of humour.

'You could have fooled me. So tell me, Sara, if you're unwilling to renew our releationship, why does your body respond to mine as if you were made for me?'

'You imagine that, Drew. You and I have been on separate paths for too long now. I came here to try to come to some formal understanding about this separation. It's you who have forced me into this situation. I didn't ask to come here and I have no intention of renewing our relationship, as you put it, just because I find myself alone with you in this forsaken place.'

'Oh, but you will, Sara. When you've been here for a few days, here in this wonderful African wilderness, you'll begin to love it almost as much as I do, I promise you, and you'll learn to love me too. Soon you'll be like the lioness, begging for her lord's favours.'

She could hardly resist the enchantment of his smile, but she held herself rigidly as he put out a hand and shook her shoulder lightly.

'The lioness is always willing, just as you will be when you've forgotten those lost years. Go to sleep now. It would be easy to take you now, but I intend you should confess to me that you want it too. Tomorrow is another day.'

CHAPTER EIGHT

WHEN Sara awoke, the first glimmer of greyish light was filtering secretly into the narrow slotlike windows of the hunting lodge. She was on the mattress in front of the hearth and the fire was still glowing. Drew must have made it up during the night, and he must have put this blanket over her too. She needed it now, because it was chilly here with the mattress placed directly on to the tiled floor, but out in the wilderness it would be hot as soon as the sun rose. She must get up quietly and do as she had decided the night before. Certainly she could not stay, for if she did, she knew she would be involved with Drew as she had been before. But this time she was a mature woman and now she knew she must avoid a new relationship with him. A few days' enchantment followed by months of heartbreak—no, that was not for her, not this time around.

Drew was still sound asleep only a few feet away from her. He had taken off his shirt and his naked torso showed golden-brown above the cream of the blanket. He must have risen earlier to renew the fire and now had fallen into what looked like a sound slumber. Asleep like that he looked younger, more vulnerable. It was hard to resist the feeling of tender passion that welled up in her at the sight of his sleeping face, but Sara told herself that was just some relic of the distant past. Now she must be strong for both of them and get away from here. It was madly dangerous and crazy for Drew to think they could stay in this wild place for any length of time, even putting aside the fact that he intended they should have this 'short affair' while they were here.

She knew where he had placed the car key on the deep mantel above the fireplace. She would take it and drive back to the camp, then return with Clive, who

115

might be better at persuading Drew to return. Drew had brought extra petrol and it had been left in the car, but she did not think she would need it. She would just have to trust that Drew would not do anything foolish while she was away. She could be back by evening at the latest. This, she thought, was the best thing to do. She must escape. Even the idea came to her that she could leave Clive to come here by himself and she need have no further part in it. Suppose she were to go before they came back, never see him again. That would be a very sensible thing to do . . . and yet . . . and yet . . .

As she opened the door, it gave a loud creak. She glanced at Drew and saw that he had stirred. If she closed it and it gave an equally loud noise, he would be bound to wake. She would have to leave it open; she was sure he would be awake very soon. He would probably hear the noise of the car, but she hoped by that time she could get away. Outside, the air had a kind of blueness and the dawn light was coming fast. Wakening birds were beginning to murmur to each other and she saw the red back of a jackal streaking away in the distance, sleek and neat like some satisfied male coming home from his date.

For the first time ever Sara had a faint feeling of harmony with her surroundings here. Seen like this in the early morning, the wilderness was beautiful. She had a sudden sense of wellbeing, as if even she could begin to enjoy her surroundings. But it's just the usual feeling of being up early in the morning, she told herself. Well, at least I don't feel frightened of the journey ahead of me which I must make entirely on my own. She realised that she had never been alone in the wilderness before. Drew had always protected her so much from contact with the realities of the reserve—maybe too much so.

And now at this late stage he was willing she should know more about it, but it was too late. She had made her choice three years ago when she had left him. There was no retracing her steps. Forget how you felt last night when he put his hand on your breast, she told herself. He doesn't want you back; he only wants to show he can still enchant you with his old lures.

At the top of the slope where the lodge had first come into view, she stopped the car and looked back. She did not know what made her do this, unless it was a faint hope of seeing Drew once again in the distance, but he had appeared to be sound asleep again and she had run the car down a slope a little way before starting it, so she did not really think that would have wakened him. And then it seemed as if her heart stopped beating and she felt herself go ice-cold with horror—for advancing along the road she had just left, almost level with the lodge, a group of lions ambled slowly but purposefully towards the building. To her startled eyes, they seemed to be the largest lions she had ever seen. The leader, a huge lion with a rolling gait and swinging distended belly, had a black ruff around its massive face and jaws. There was one other lion almost as large and a troop of lionesses with several cubs. They advanced on the lodge as if they owned the place—which, Sara suddenly thought, they probably did.

She remembered the rank animal smell that had alarmed her when they first entered the building. It was possible that these lions had become accustomed to treating the place as a haven, a shelter from the heat of the day in this desert place, where the small trees were so comparatively leafless that they gave little shade. They were probably accustomed to spending part of the day in the shadows cast by the walls.

The door! She had forgotten that she had left the door open in case it made a noise when she left. Now, with a lightning flash of fear, she imagined the lions entering the room where Drew must still be sleeping. She would have to turn back and she would have to face these great beasts. She could not leave Drew on his own with this terrible threat. But where to turn the car? It was on a narrow road and there was rough countryside all around. Somehow, frantically, she managed to turn it. She didn't know quite how she did it, and then she was putting her foot down hard on the accelerator as she swiftly drove towards the pride. They don't know I'm in the car, she told herself. Drew said they don't connect cars with people.

Coming to think about it, these lions probably don't even know about cars. But they know what annoys them. Anything that gets in the way of their aim and object, and in this case the object is to gain the shelter of the lodge. As she drove towards them, they looked disconcerted, then showed their annoyance in no uncertain fashion, snarling and shaking their great heads with the huge black manes. Sara expected that at any moment they would spring upon the car, but then, much to her relief, they backed away and began to make a hasty, rather undignified retreat.

But one lion, seeming slower than his companions, and finding himself left on his own, appeared to panic and, trying to find some hiding place, to Sara's horror made for the open door. By this time the other lions incredibly had vanished from her view, their gold dust pelts somehow blending in with the browns and golds of the dry landscape. There was a spade in the back of the car, and Sara got hold of it. She knew she would have to go inside the lodge and yet dreaded what she might see when she entered. Where were the other lions? How could they have disappeared from sight so successfully? Or were they waiting in some nearby bush, waiting to spring on her the moment she got out of the car?

But she would have to risk it. Drew had mentioned yesterday that he had brought a gun, but she had not seen it and did not even know where he had put it. It could not be far away. Could she get hold of it before the lion made an attack? Holding the spade like a sword, she got out of the car and advanced towards the open door. She could sense her heart shaking like a speedometer needle and her legs felt like candles. And then her trembling heart started thudding in her chest so rapidly that she felt as if she could not breathe.

Beside the fireplace on the bed on which she had left Drew sleeping peacefully, the lion had hold of something, something hidden beyond his powerful form. He had it in his mouth and was shaking it like a puppy playing with a piece of rag. Sara had come in out of the bright sunlight and now in the shadowy room she found it difficult to see. There was no sound from the bed. Had the lion already severed the jugular vein of its victim as they did to their prey in the wilds? She gave a shout that was more like a strangled scream, and the lion glanced towards her, turning its huge head with the golden glaring eyes. Her eyes had by now become adjusted to the light and she saw with an indescribable feeling of relief that the object in its mouth was the blanket, which it proceeded to tear to shreds, still keeping her in view.

But where was Drew? She was suddenly aware of a sound, the squeaking noise of an old pump being used to draw water, but before she could think what to do to warn him, the lion, seemingly having had enough of staring at her and worrying the blanket, was making its way, not towards the door and her, but in the direction of the kitchen. Now the lion was between her and the place where Drew presumably was drawing water. How could she warn him? Judging by the rest of the pride's reaction, any sudden noise would startle and annoy this beast.

When she gained the inner door of the kitchen, the lion was already disappearing out of the back door which Drew had left open. She could see Drew in the sunlight, working the handle of the pump as water wet his face and hair and showered over the brown muscles of his back in sparkling drops. She rushed towards the outer door and saw the lion walking directly towards Drew, where he stood enjoying the feel of the cool water on his shoulders, quite oblivious of any impending danger. The gun! She had forgotten to look for the gun. She ran back into the room she had must left and searched around where Drew had placed their few possessions. Scrabbling frantically in his packbag, she was certain that at any moment she would hear the sound of the lion's attack, but all she heard was the sound of the pump, the monotonous squeak as it was lifted up and down.

No, she could not find the gun, and if she did how could she use it without injuring Drew, she who had not handled a gun for years? Again with beating heart she ran to the door, seizing a heavy fireiron as she went. The lion now was within two yards of Drew, and some sixth sense made him swing around. They stood, man and beast, staring at each other—at least it looked like that to Sara, but how much could Drew see? The lion was so close that he must be able to see it if only in grey outline. The rank smell of the animal wafted to Sara as she stood trembling at the door. It must be very strong where Drew was standing. Then from somewhere in the bushes to the left of the lodge, there came the sound of a sudden fracas, like the squabbling of enormous cats. The lion hesitated, then turned around, forgetting his interest in the strange man, and swiftly made his way towards his fellows. From where she was standing, Sara could see the group of them, having forgotten their short squabble for the present, ambling lazily along the road. They seemed to have given up any idea of using the lodge for shelter.

She ran to Drew, who was standing there still, his shining golden skin covered with trickling drops of water, his head wet and dark as a seal's. Heedless of the wetness, she clung to him trembling and sobbing, and he held her, not saying anything at first, waiting until the storm of emotion calmed a little.

'Did you see it?' she gasped when she was able to speak.

'I saw the lion, yes. Anything as big as that appears in my field of vision, certainly.'

'But weren't you afraid?'

'Not particularly. These lions don't know anything about man. Obviously they're as curious as cats. But I knew there could be very little danger. I could see by its outline, and its huge swinging belly, that it must have eaten very recently. Truly , Sara, there was no danger to either of us. I must admit it feels good to have you clinging to me for a change instead of sending me away, but if it's all on account of one curious lion, I can't see that it needs so much emotion.'

Sara drew away from him.

'You make me mad! How can you be so calm about it? There was a whole pride of lions just about to go into the lodge when I disturbed them. And that one came inside. It worried the blanket. I thought ... I thought ...'

In spite of her resistance, Drew took her in his arms again, then he moved towards the house stroking her as if, she thought indignantly, she were a highly strung pony.

'You thought it was me. Oh, Sara, you should know after all these years that I take a lot of killing!'

'Oh, I know you have some illusion that you lead a kind of charmed life. You always have had it—but, Drew, don't be so sure. You're no St Francis, even if you think you are.'

They were in the cool kitchen now, away from the rising heat of the outside world. Drew flung his head back and laughed, not mockingly but with genuine amusement.

'No, Sara, I must admit you're right. I am no saint, certainly. But good lord, you ought to know that I've lived in association with lions for most of the adult part of my life. I'm used to them and they don't scare me. Certainly I respect them, but most of the time they don't wish man any harm unless he gets in their way. They much prefer a diet of nice plump zebra or springbok. You should know that.'

'I don't know it,' said Sara crossly. 'I only know that by coming here you've placed yourself and me in a quite unnecessary situation of risk. I insist that you should go back. You're insane to think I'd stay here after this! I was all set to go back when this happened. I wish now that I'd left you to the wretched lions—you deserve it!'

'So—you were about to leave me,' he drawled. 'In fact you had left me. How far would you have got, do you think, before your conscience would have forced you to turn back?'

'Where you're concerned, I haven't got a conscience.'

'I don't believe you. You came back to me now.'

'Only because I saw the lions. Otherwise I intended to go and fetch Clive and see if he could talk any sense into you.'

'Oh, Sara, Sara, how can I convince you that at the moment this is the very best thing for me?' sighed Drew. 'I need to be on my own away from the other fellows in the camp, but I'm not so crazy as to think I can manage without a bit of help, and that's where you come in.'

'What makes you think I'm willing to go along with this? Quite frankly, I'm not. I want out of this, and the sooner the better!'

'Calm down,' he said firmly. 'You're in a highly emotional state at the moment. One would think you'd had never seen lions before. If you're to live here for a while, you'll have to get used to the fact that the wilderness belongs to the animals. Only man is the intruder.'

'Well, if man is the intruder, Drew, what, may I ask, are we doing here?' Sara demanded.

'Good question. We're here because I want to be. Because the wilderness can do something for me that nothing else can at this time. Not even the love of a beautiful woman, although I'm more than willing to test that theory.'

'That's just it! Understand this, Drew—I am not willing to go along with any of your crazy ideas. I'm not willing to consort with lions, as you seem to expect, and even more so, I'm not willing to have this short affair that you seem to think can improve your health. Well, it won't improve mine, I know. So just count me out. I'm going back to the main camp today. Perhaps I can persuade Maxine to come here. Who knows?'

'Just at the moment it's you I need, not Maxine. If she came here in such a setting she would be too much concentrated upon her profession. And as I said, she would need to bring her assistants. No, Sara, I brought you because I needed someone whose sole interest could be concentrated upon me.'

'Well, now I've heard everything! You certainly have one high opinion of yourself, Drew. What makes you think I could be willing to devote myself entirely to your needs? Specially considering that I came here unwillingly in the first place. You always were a self-opinionated, arrogant man when we were married, and three years of being a bachelor again certainly hasn't made any improvement!'

They had been standing apart glaring at each other like two angry cats, but now Drew came towards her and swept her into his arms. Before she could attempt to free herself, his mouth travelled over the shape of her face, seeking hers, and those firm lips she had once known so well were upon them, forcing them apart demanding their surrender.

When he let her go, he was smiling.

'That seems to be the only way to stop your criticism of me, Sara. It works, doesn't it? When are you going to admit that we still have a lot going for us? If only you would follow what your body tells you to do, we could both enjoy a short stay in paradise.'

'You have an odd idea of paradise!' she snapped. 'Well, Drew, now I'm here, I may as well wash. Do I have to use the outside pump?'

He was still smiling in that way that she had learned not to trust, but he shook his head and sounded quite amiable as he told her, 'Not at all. Didn't I tell you that the Baron used to bring his mistresses here on occasion? There's a luxury shower room en suite with the bedroom, and it even has gold taps—if no one has rustled them in the meantime. However, for the time being you'll have to manage with cold water, I'm afraid. The hot water supply is a spot old-fashioned. It needs stoking, and that we can attempt later.'

'You mean you can,' retorted Sara. 'I won't be needing hot water. There's plenty in the main camp.'

Drew made no reply to this as he showed her up to the bathroom on the next floor.

'You really did think of everything, didn't you?' she told him as he handed her a large fluffy bath towel.

'Goodness,' she exclaimed, when she saw the size of the bathroom, 'you could hold a party here!'

'Probably the Baron did. Rather private parties, I suspect.'

'Yes, I see what you mean.'

The enormous bath was in the shape of a shell and was made of pink marble. All the fittings, taps, rails and shower arrangements were gold decorated with intricate patterns. On the walls were decorations in mosaic. One showed Venus rising from the waves and there were pictures of nymphs being pursued by satyrs. The nymphs, thought Sara, did not look particularly alarmed. The whole of the ceiling and the walls were mirrored, dull and faded now, but when new they must have been brilliant.

'I've checked that the plumbing works,' said Drew. 'There's plenty of water from the spring. Enjoy yourself.'

And with that he left her. This place gets more and more curious, thought Sara, when she had settled herself into the tepid water of the bath. It was not at all cold, but she found it very refreshing. She still felt shaken when she remembered the pride of lions and was convinced that the best thing for both of them would be to get out of here quickly. But how to persuade Drew? He seemed so determined to stay, lions or not. But she herself was equally determined to go, especially when she remembered the effect of his kiss. If I stay here I'll be lost, she told herself. How can I resist this insane attraction that he still has for me when he takes me in his arms? And he knows it. He can tell he has this power over me; that's why he brought me here. But I'm not staying. I must get away from here, and the quicker the better.

With this thought she got out of the beautiful bath and dried herself on the fluffy towel. Drew had brought her suitcase up to the Baron's bedroom and she dressed herself amid all the faded splendour of this romantic place. As she brushed her hair in front of the dim glass of the gilded mirror, at the splendid dressing table, she wondered what other women had seen their reflection here in this place that the Baron had built in such strange surroundings. How could they have borne to stay here? And yet if they had loved him? And then there would have been other people here, she supposed, a whole bevy of servants, people to cook for them in the huge kitchen, people to help the Baron's mistress dress her hair, prepare her bath after the day's hunting. Did they hunt too? she wondered. Or did the women spend the day doing feminine things, embroidering, playing the card games that were popular while the men went out shooting? They must have needed courage to stay here, she thought, more courage than I have.

She wound her red-gold hair high on her head away from her neck and dressed in blue and pink striped slacks and a pale pink shirt in thin cotton material. If Drew had to kidnap her it was just as well she had had her suitcase with her. But I won't need any more clothes for staying here, she thought, because as soon as I'm ready I'll be on my way.

When she came downstairs, she could hear that he was busy in the kitchen, and when she entered she saw that he had placed eggs, bacon and sausages on the old table.

'I suppose you're expecting I'll cook that?' she remarked.

'Not especially. Even with only half my sight, I can still manage to make quite a good job of this. Years of practice in the wilderness. Cooking breakfast is second nature to me.'

'I thought you always used to take a cook with you. That's what you told me when I said I could come and do the cooking on these expeditions.'

'Not always. Let's say I was just putting you off. Truly, Sara, you never seemed suitable in those days for adventures in the bush,' Drew added.

'And what makes you think I'm suitable now?'

'I don't think so, but needs must. Besides, as I've told

you before, I didn't bring you here just for cooking, nor for risky adventures in the wilderness. I brought you for, shall we say, a different kind of adventure.'

'You mean the kind for which the Baron brought his mistresses,' Sara said coldly.

'Perhaps.'

How well she knew that wicked smile below the veiled eyes. It had often made her angry before and it made her angry now.

'But I'm my own mistress, never anyone else's. And I don't go in for short affairs, even with you, Drew, or should I say, more especially with you, who couldn't even succeed as my husband!'

She had aroused his anger now. The smile had vanished and she felt a sense of triumph mixed with a thrill of fear. He strode over to where she stood and grasped her roughly by the shoulders. It seemed almost as if he could hardly restrain himself from shaking her.

'And what do you mean by that remark?' he demanded.

'I meant that both of us know our marriage failed.'

'And you put the entire blame on me?'

'Not altogether. I guess I had some faults too.'

'I'm glad you admit it,' he grated. 'You were young, certainly, but you knew how to arouse a man's anger and jealousy, as certainly you still do.'

Sara tore herself from his bruising grasp.

'That was because you always were damned unreasonable! You left me alone while you went into the wilderness. How could you not expect that other men might take advantage of that?'

'Other men such as Brad? And he can still grasp his opportunity, can't he? He very quickly decided to visit you in your room the other night. How much encouragement had he had, I wonder, before you changed your mind and decided he was not welcome?'

'And if I'd decided that he was welcome, what had it to do with you, Drew, at this late stage? No, really, Drew, you're still the same arrogant unreasonable man I married. I should never have come back, let alone found myself in this situation. And I'm getting out of it right now. You can cook your own breakfast!'

Sara flew up to the room and flung in the few clothes she had unpacked, then came down carrying her suitcase without asking for Drew's help. He was still in the kitchen, using the gas cooker he had brought, and turning over the pieces of sizzling bacon, the picture of domesticity. For some reason this angered her even more.

'Goodbye. When I get there I'll send Clive to talk some sense into you.'

'Do that,' he shrugged. 'Perhaps he'll join me for a bit of lion research. I haven't been on an expedition into the wilderness with old Clive in ages.'

'I don't think old Clive will be interested in your expeditions. He'll persuade you to come back to the camp.'

'Oh, I don't know. He knows I take some persuading to do otherwise when I've made my own plans.'

He sounded very tranquil, quite different from the angry man of a little while ago. He seemed to be letting her go very easily—but perhaps he had decided, as she had, that the whole thing had been a mistake. Well, he would have to take his chance with the lions for today. Perhaps, if she made good time, Clive could get here before dark. She had definitely decided that she would not come back. Clive would know the way here, and meanwhile she could make arrangements to leave the camp before they returned. Yes, definitely, this was the best way.

'I'll carry that out for you,' Drew offered.

'No, don't bother,' she said sharply. 'I wouldn't dream of interfering with your cooking.'

'You're going to be hungry before you've got very far. Won't you stay for breakfast?'

The smell of the bacon and sausages was wafting towards her and the coffee perking on the other ring, fragrant and tempting, but she resisted it.

'No, thank you. I haven't got time if I'm to arrive there by afternoon. I'll take a packet of biscuits and a bottle of soda water.'

'Yes, do that. Well, goodbye, have a good journey.'

He turned his back on her, getting on with his domestic task and looking, she thought, totally unconcerned that she was going out on her own into the wilderness. But what else could she expect?

He might at least have insisted on coming to the car with me, she thought, as she looked fearfully at the bushes to see if there were any animals hiding there, but the sun was high now and all the beasts of the wilderness were quiet. Only a dove sang its monotonous song on the branch of a tomboti tree, 'My children are dead, my father is dead, my mother is dead and so I go doo-doo-doo.' Her nanny had told her that very long ago.

She put her case into the boot and settled herself in the driver's seat, then turned the ignition key. Silence. Surely the engine could not be cold in this climate? Sara pulled out the choke and tried again. She heard the engine turn, but there was no answering spark. She turned the engine over once again. No response. She sat there desperately trying to coax some life out of the obstinate mechanism. The noise of the turning engine, chug-chugging with no answering purr, had chased away the dove but had not brought Drew away from his breakfast. Why didn't he come to help her? But she could hardly expect it, she supposed. After struggling for the best part of fifteen minutes, she wearily gave up and went back into the lodge.

Drew was sitting at the table, calmly eating a plate of bacon and eggs and sausages.

'Back so soon?' he asked. 'More lions?'

'Of course not!' she blazed at him. 'You know very well I've never been away—the car won't start!'

'Really? And it's usually so reliable. Perhaps it objects to being driven by a woman.'

'Well, it didn't before.'

He shook his head.

'Very strange. I can't understand it.'

'Well, can't you come and do something about it instead of sitting there so smugly?' she cried, feeling thoroughly exasperated.

'Sit down and have some breakfast,' invited Drew. 'There's plenty here for two. Then, when I have the strength, I'll come and see what I can do.'

Reluctantly Sara sat down and accepted a plate of bacon and eggs and a cup of coffee. It was beautifully cooked. She wondered how he could be so expert when he could hardly see; he must do it by timing. They ate in silence and she accepted another cup of coffee impatiently because he insisted that he needed another cup.

'Now please won't you come?' she pleaded when at last he had finished.

'You certainly are in a hurry to leave me,' he commented. 'All right. I expect it's something very simple that's gone wrong.'

When he sat in the driver's seat, she half hoped and half feared that it would start first go for Drew, but that didn't happen.

'Could the battery be flat?' she asked.

'No, it's a new battery, and anyway, the engine wouldn't turn if it was the battery.'

'Could it be the coil?'

'You seem to have quite a working knowledge of engines,' he commented. 'Yes, no doubt it could be the coil. Let's have a look.'

He seemed to Sara to take a long time with his head inside the bonnet before he turned to her and said, 'Yes, Sara, you're right, as usual. It is the coil that's packed up and therefore we aren't getting any spark.'

'So what's to be done?'

Drew shook his head. A small smile played about his lips.

'Not much. We haven't got a spare coil.'

'So then we're stuck here?'

'It looks like it.'

'But how can you be so calm? What are we to do? No one knows we're here. We could be stuck here for ever!'

'True. But don't you mean what are you to do? I'm quite happy here. I had no intention of moving at least until the rains come, and you know even the rains can get delayed here for seven years.'

'How can you joke about it? Here we are with no transport, left in the wilderness completely helpless, and it's all your fault!' she exclaimed.

'Not completely helpless, surely? We have plenty of food and if we show any signs of running out of tins, I have a gun and plenty of ammunition. We have a water supply and even plenty of wine. We can last out here for ever, Robinson Crusoe and his Girl Friday. How do you go for that?'

'You know very well I don't go for it at all—and if you think this is going to change my mind about having what you call an affair with you, you can forget it! If you were the last man in the world, I'd refuse to have anything to do with you, feeling as angry as I do with you now!'

'As far as the present situation goes, I'm the last man in the world, and soon, Sara, very, very soon, you're going to change your mind. You were mine once and you'll be mine again—I know it.'

'Well, I don't, and I've changed my mind about sleeping in the Baron's bedroom because I've noticed it has a nice large key in the door and I intend to use it,' Sara told him.

'How do you know you won't succumb to temptation in quite a different setting? The wilderness could be our garden of Eden, Sara.'

'Not mine,' said Sara adamantly. 'Just count me out of your schemes, Drew.'

CHAPTER NINE

'WELL, you can't sit and sulk here for the next seven years, can you, Sara? How say we go and explore our country?'

'I expect I have no choice,' Sara shrugged. 'I certainly don't want to be left here on my own to face those lions again. Do you think they really regard this as their home?'

'They may have become used to using it for shelter. I wouldn't worry too much about it. They dislike our smell as much as we dislike theirs. Once they realise we've established ourselves here, my guess would be that they'll avoid it.'

'I hope you're right. So what are you proposing to do next?' she asked.

'I'm suggesting that we should walk in the wilderness.'

'*Walk*? What, among all those lions, not to mention elephants, cheetahs and black rhinos?'

'Don't be alarmed,' he reassured her. 'Roaming the country is the true way to explore Africa, as David Livingstone proved before me. The early explorers came to very little harm from the animals around them, and neither need we.'

'But, Drew, how can we? I mean, what about your ...'

'My eyesight? Look, Sara, I've often done this kind of thing at night when one is hampered by darkness. This that I have is no worse than that—better, in fact. I can still see objects even if they do appear colourless and I still have very keen hearing and sense of smell. Trust me. The experience of years will count against this temporary handicap.'

Sara wanted to ask how he could be so sure it was temporary, but she did not dare. They certainly were in a difficult situation now and she must not do anything to impair his confidence. Although there doesn't seem much likelihood of that, she said to herself. Now he's away from the camp and feels independent again, there seems to be no holding him.

'But what are we to do about the car?' she asked. 'Could we make our way back to one of the main roads on foot?'

'What for? I'm quite happy here. And you will be quite soon, I assure you. Just like a woman to be so contradictory! One moment you complain that I never took you on my travels in the wilderness and the next you complain if I do.'

'There are a few differences between now and then, Drew. When I wanted to accompany you, I was married to you. I was young and I was . . .'

She hesitated, and he supplied the word.

'In love. And that is gone now, has it, Sara? Vanished like those mirages of another world that you see across the dryness of the Pan.'

'You know it has,' she said.

He shrugged.

'I suppose so.'

Then why did you bring me here? she wanted to demand. What sense was there in thinking you could revive physical feelings that you knew couldn't even last?

'We'll walk along the dry river beds,' he said now, instantly dismissing the subject of love as if it had no more importance to him. 'That will give us pleasant walking. We'll find trees there that will give us shade and we may see some of the animals taking their noonday rests. How does that grab you?'

'So long as you're sure they will be resting,' Sara said doubtfully.

'I can assure you most animals don't get active until much later when they need to drink and look for food. We'll have the wilderness to ourselves for most of the day. You saw that for yourself yesterday.'

'Yes, I suppose I did.'

'There's no need at all to feel nervous when you're out in the wilderness,' Drew told her. 'On the other hand, you must keep constantly on the alert. Remember the country belongs to the wild life here, and not to you.'

'You don't have to tell me!'

I'm not only on the alert, she thought, as they set off from the lodge. I'm completely petrified. But what was the alternative to going with Drew? Staying behind and wondering what was happening to him alone, with damaged eyesight, in this savage country.

Drew seemed to know his way around here. It wasn't long before they came to a dry river bed that was bordered by fairly tall trees that, as he had said, gave very welcome shade. The river bed was sandy but not difficult for walking. The first time a large animal arose suddenly from the shade almost at their feet, Sara felt as if her heart had stopped. But it was only a large antelope, disturbed by them from its siesta. It gave a loud warning bark and other animals got up hurriedly and clattered over the rocks. In the deep shade they had been hardly visible, but now Sara could see their tawny pelts glistening in the light of the hot sun.

'They're such a beautiful colour,' she told Drew.

'Unfortunately not to me. They're just grey shapes—but graceful nevertheless.'

Small antelope that they came across seemed less alarmed at their presence. They stood upon the rocks gazing at them with large eyes, curious as cats, then darted away with dainty leaps. Up above them on the highest points of the cliffs baboons shouted, warning them off their territory, and rock rabbits called to each other, secure on their perches, basking in the sun like bathers in the South of France. Sara began to feel more at ease. When they came to open glades where the trees were not so numerous, the light was dazzling and the air quivered with waves of heat, but in the shade of the trees there was a welcome breeze.

Drew seemed in his element. He strode along, his face towards the wind, alert to every sound and smell. He hardly spoke to Sara, and she knew that this was best. She herself felt that she must be doubly on the alert, because she had to be the eyes for both of them. He had brought a rucksack with a flask of coffee and a pack of hard tack, biltong which was a kind of dried meat, rye biscuits, raisins, oranges and dried bananas. They climbed a little kopje, a small hill nearby that must have had some soil among its huge granite boulders, for there was a leadwood tree growing with its light grey striped bark and its leaves affording deep shade from the heat of the afternoon. It was good to rest there and drink the reviving coffee.

'It wouldn't have been any good bringing cold drinks or beer,' Drew commented. 'It would only have been tepid by now. Oh, Sara, this is the life, don't you feel it? Cars are all very well, but walking is the only way to see the wilderness properly. I can feel Africa coming up through the soles of my feet. How do you feel now?'

'I feel I'm a long way from Paris,' said Sara.

His face, which had been turned towards her with that engaging smile she knew so well, darkened as if a cloud had passed over the sun.

'Yes, you appear to have made another life for yourself very successfully,' he agreed.

'I have, but if I don't get back in time, there won't be any of that life left for me. Madame is a hard taskmaster. She doesn't take kindly to delay.'

'We'll get back all in good time, never fear.'

'But how?'

'Stop thinking about it. The only important time is here and now. Forget any other world exists. This could be our world, Sara, if for a little while you could stop fretting and forget everything else. This wilderness is yours and mine. Nothing else matters.'

'But it does, Drew. We can't turn back the clock even if we wanted to. The life we had together is in the past. We had our chance then and we couldn't make a go of it. There's no future for people like us.'

'But there's a present.'

His hands were on her shoulders and he was pressing

her back on to the handwoven grass mat he had
brought. She could smell its fragrance, wild and sweet,
the smell of Africa. Beyond his shoulders she saw a
lizard, brilliant blue and orange, scuttle across a rock,
then sit motionless watching them with brilliant jewels
for eyes.

Drew was seeking her mouth, his lips feeling the
smooth lines of her face and, with senses stirring, she
could not turn away from him. A small pulse began to
quiver at the base of her throat and she knew that she
must submit to the trembling ecstasy that was invading
her being. His hands slid under the thin cotton of her
shirt and her back felt shudderingly smooth beneath his
caresses. She was back in the past now, however much
she might protest, and his kisses were at once familiar
and yet strange. Caught up against the warm hardness
of his body, she felt again the old blazing rapture that
had so often overwhelmed every sense except the desire
to be held closer, closer.

I'm lost, she thought, as I knew I would be if I
stayed. In spite of the gap of time and distance, he can
still arouse in me such soul-stirring ecstasy that I forget
everything else.

'Now don't you see?' he muttered. 'We could be in
paradise for a while. The world forgetting, by the world
forgot. We know it won't last, but while it does, let's
follow this desire.'

His lips were on hers again, but this time he gave her
a slow languorous kiss that seemed to suit the warm
sensuous atmosphere of the African day, and his hand
was cupping her breast caressing it with seductive
gentleness. She felt herself being carried away on the
heady currents of sensual passion, and she had
forgotten her promise to herself to be constantly on the
alert when she was with him in this wild country, but
out there in the shimmering light of noon, nothing
stirred. Only the bright lizards wove their green bodies
up and down as if doing perpetual press-ups and there
was the chirring sound of grasshoppers from the bushes
nearby.

Then, suddenly, so close that it made them start away from each other with fast beating hearts, there was a crashing sound through the bushes and, only a few feet away from them, as Sara sat up, startled and alarmed, a leopard sauntered past them, then stopped and looked at them with cold green gaze before disappearing into the bushes on the other side of the clearing.

'You know what that was, don't you?' Sara turned on Drew accusingly.

'Certainly I do. I could tell by the smell even if it hadn't been so close. You don't often see a leopard by daylight. We should consider ourselves fortunate.'

'Fortunate?' she echoed. 'Now I really do think you're crazy! Why, it must have been very close to us all this time. Anything could have happened!'

'But it didn't, did it? It was as surprised at the sight of us as we were by it. It probably hides up among these rocks in daylight hours, but it didn't relish the idea of spending any more time so close to us. It must have been watching us for quite a long time.'

'I doubt whether it can have appreciated what it saw.'

Sara spoke crossly, but Drew laughed out loud and stretched himself so that she could see his muscles rippling under the bronze skin just as the leopard's had moved beneath the gold of its pelt.

'Not to worry. It can't tell any tales, but it certainly interrupted us at the wrong moment, you must admit.'

'I'm not sure that I do. I have a feeling I should be grateful to that leopard.'

'There'll be a better time, a better place, you'll see. Now let's catch a little rest before we go on. I know of a waterhole near here that should be worth visiting later.'

'But what if the leopard comes back?' queried Sara.

'It won't. It was as scared of you as you were of it. It has by now found some other hiding place where it hopes it won't be interrupted by the eccentric behaviour of the human race. Take the rucksack for a pillow and stop worrying. Nothing else will stir for an hour or two. It's time for a siesta.'

With this Drew closed his eyes and, in what seemed

like a few seconds, she could tell by his breathing that he was asleep. She remembered that he had always had this knack of instant slumber, so now he must definitely be feeling more relaxed than he had been at the camp, where he seemed to spend hours of the night wakeful and restless near the waterhole.

The interruption to their lovemaking hardly seemed to have worried him. Was that because he felt sure that before very long she would agree to his wish to spend this time here as lovers? That was the remedy the German doctor had suggested, wasn't it? But that was nonsense. If she let herself be carried away by Drew's lovemaking as she had done just now, in the end there must be even worse heartbreak than she had suffered previously.

She looked at his sleeping face, so relaxed and now innocent of the maddening smile he so often had when he was teasing her. This may be what the doctor ordered for you, she admonished him silently, but it's not doing me any good. That wretched car! Why did it have to go wrong just at this time? If it hadn't been for that, I could have been miles away from here by now, travelling back to civilisation instead of having to encounter leopards in the company of a man who wants to have a short affair with his own wife for therapeutic reasons.

Where is this all leading me? she thought. Away from the life I'd so carefully made for myself? But no, Drew doesn't intend this present association should mean any more to him than a casual affair with any pretty girl. Anyone would have done for his purpose, so long as they could keep up with him, both in traversing the wilderness and in making love. But why didn't he bring Maxine? I guess because she has more sense and because he needed someone he thought he could subjugate to his will. And that means me. Oh, no, Drew, you must think again.

I slipped up in my determination just now, but it mustn't happen again. In future I must remember to avoid close encounters in the heat of the afternoon, or at any other time for that matter. But I know too well it's not going to be easy. When he's made up his mind about something, Drew is like an irresistible force running down all opposition. I just mustn't let myself be overwhelmed by that ravishing attraction. She had thought she could not sleep, so disturbed had she been by the sighting of the leopard, but, in the drowsy heat of the afternoon, in spite of her determination to keep alert, she felt her lids grow heavy. When she awoke, she saw Drew's face above her. His expression was strange, difficult to interpret. Sara remained quite still wondering how clearly he could see her, but he must have sensed in some way that she was awake. Perhaps her breathing had quickened.

'Did you have a good sleep?' he asked.

'Wonderful,' she said before she could stop herself.

She had not intended to let him know how good it felt to awake again and be aware of his presence. It was like one of those dreams that had so often plagued her in Paris, but this time he didn't vanish with the daylight. His smile had a spark of triumph in it.

'That's my girl! We'll make a wilderness ranger of you yet!'

The delicious haziness of sleep was vanishing now in the reality of her situation.

'Don't you think it's a little late for that, Drew? You should have tried harder in the early days. You might have succeeded then, but not now.'

'We'll see. Come on, the sun is getting low, and if we're to watch at the waterhole for a while and then make our way back to the lodge by sunset, we'd better get moving.'

All Sara's fears came back again as they began to move on along the dry river bed and then along a path that led, Drew told her, to the waterhole.

'Will there be lions there?' she asked.

'It's possible, but we'll stay downwind of them. However, I doubt whether there'll be much big game at this time of day. Maybe the odd rhino.'

'That's consoling,' said Sara with sarcasm. 'Just what I've always wanted—the opportunity to meet a rhino on foot.'

'Well, if you do, especially if it's a black rhino, you'd better climb up the nearest tree. They're ugly customers if you happen to cross their path. But not to worry, rhinos aren't especially prevalent in this area.'

'That's a relief,' said Sara dryly.

'Of course, dry river beds are a favourite spot for them if there do happen to be any about,' added Drew.

'Now you tell me!'

'I didn't want a rebellion on my hands.'

'You've got it,' she assured him, 'whether you want it or not.'

'It's an enchanting waterhole, I promise you.'

'It had better be!'

When they came to it, Sara had to admit that he was right. It was bordered by tall tamboti trees and there was an island in the middle where tall reeds grew. They approached quietly and cautiously, and Drew motioned her to hide beside him in a bush nearby.

'The wind is blowing towards us,' he whispered. 'They shouldn't get our scent.'

At the edge of the pool, its legs splayed out in an awkward-looking stance, there was a huge giraffe lapping vigorously at the water. Zebra and wildebeest swallowed avidly and then at some small sound wheeled agitatedly away, only to reform in a few seconds and begin their drinking again. Above the pool, yellow-billed kites wheeled in the sunlit air, catching flying insects. Drew seemed to have some sixth sense that told him what was going on. Of course these bigger animals were not difficult to see, even if the scene was only vague to him, but he seemed anxious that Sara should appreciate every aspect of the pool.

'I can hear the sand-grouse now,' he said. 'They must by flying in for water.'

'Yes, I can see some kind of bird landing, something like a pigeon.'

'That's it. You must notice how they soak their breast feathers in the water. That way they carry water back to their young.'

A kudu with majestic spiral horns stalked with dignity towards the water.

'It's amazing how animals suddenly appear. It's like magic,' Sara said.

Gemsbok came too, with strange black and white faces and long spearlike horns.

'Early travellers thought they were the fabled unicorn,' Drew told her.

She wanted to ask how much he could actually see. The bigger animals must appear in outline to him, but was he depending very much on scent and hearing?

A hawk dropped like a stone to seize one of the sand-grouse and birds swarmed up in a cloud of fluttering wings. The animals took fright as well. Warthogs sprang up from their wallowing in the mud and the antelopes and zebras leaped away in panic while the giraffe ran for cover with a slow rocking horse action.

'They're constantly on the alert, as we must be too,' said Drew.

'Don't I know it!' said Sara wryly.

'If any lion is watching, he'll have to wait a little longer now.'

'You don't really think there is a lion hidden in those little bushes over there?' asked Sara nervously.

'Could be. The largest lion, and they're very large here, can conceal himself in an incredibly small bit of vegetation. But, as I've told you before, they usually hunt at night or with the dawn, not in the heat of the afternoon. We'll come here again in the early morning,' promised Drew, as if he were offering a child a favourite treat. 'Then you may see a kill.'

'I could do without that,' said Sara.

As they made their way back, the heat had lifted a little, but Sara found that this homeward journey was even more trying to her nerves. She was constantly aware of rustling sounds among the dead leaves in the clearings. If a bird flew upwards with warning shouts, she started back, expecting at any moment to run into a rhino or a lion, but she saw only springboks leaping in startled flight away from them, and once a honey badger scuttled past. A troop of zebra thundered away from their sheltering glade, irritably neighing to each other, and red dust rose around them shimmering in the evening light.

'Sunset is Africa's best time,' said Drew. 'That and early dawn.'

But as Sara saw the fiery globe of the sun slipping swiftly down to the horizon, she thought with dread of the night before her, not only because of all the unknown creatures that inhabited the wilderness and would make themselves heard in the hours of darkness but also because she would have to face another night alone with Drew and his persuasive charm.

CHAPTER TEN

SARA bathed again in the Baron's shell-shaped bath. She was glad to wash the dust and heat of the day away, and she decided that she could have a change from the eternal slacks and find one of her dresses to wear for the evening meal. Perhaps it merited a bit of dressing up, because she had seen Drew search out a bottle of wine and take it out to place in the spring outside the house to get cool.

'I shouldn't try to look beautiful for him,' she admonished herself as she applied some make-up in front of the faded mirror. Nevertheless she carefully smudged a little azure eye-shadow above her dark blue eyes and put a rose lipstick to her mouth. And then she thought, how stupid I am! Of course it doesn't make any difference whether I use make-up or not, because he sees me all in black and greys. How odd. Why am I doing it, then? I guess it's for my own sake. All the same, I'll give him some kind of treat—I'll find my best French perfume. As she sparingly scented the sensitive pulse places of her body, she assured herself that she was just doing it for herself as much as for Drew. I deserve some luxury in this wild place, she told herself. Then she put on the rainbow dress she had worn before. It was beautifully cut and its light draperies clung to her body yet lifted lightly away from her as she walked. Again she thought, I'm doing this for me, not Drew. Probably he won't even notice that I've changed.

But he too had changed from his dusty shorts and shirt. Sara had heard the outside pump working the shower, and he appeared to her in dark slacks and a cream shirt that emphasised the deep bronze of his skin.

'There seem to be delicious smells coming from the kitchen,' she commented.

'Yes, I can still open a tin or two,' he said. 'But the

fragrance around here doesn't come from the cooking. I'm flattered that you think me worth such expensive scent, Sara.'

'Not for you,' she hastened to tell him. 'For me, to keep up my morale.'

'Poor Sara, are you missing Paris so much?'

'Of course. As you told me often enough in the old days, I'm not cut out for life in the wilderness.'

'You seemed to do pretty well today,' he commented.

Sara was surprised at the little flicker of pride that she felt as he said this. So he hadn't thought she was too cowardly? But he didn't realise what went on inside her, did he?

'Needs must,' she told him.

'Shall I finish the quotation? "Needs must when the devil drives." Am I the devil, Sara?'

As she looked at him, his bronze aquiline features made even darker by the contrast of the cream shirt, his brows dark and curving above the green-gold glittering eyes that were almost black now in the light of the lamp, she thought that there was something of the devil about him.

'I think there is something Satanic about you,' she said.

He laughed. 'Well, you told me before I was no saint. So it follows, doesn't it?'

Again Drew had lit a fire with old dried logs that he had found there and he had set a table in the middle of the room. Sara viewed the gold candlesticks with astonishment.

'Where on earth did you find those?' she asked.

'In the old chest where the Baron presumably kept his valuables. They were wrapped in a springbok skin and someone must evidently have overlooked them. Good thing they're gold and not silver, because they would have become black.'

'It seems a bit exaggerated to dine out of tins with gold candlesticks on the table,' Sara commented.

'Wait until I serve the dinner,' said Drew. 'Then you can criticise my table arrangements.'

'If you're setting the scene for a seduction, you're wasting your time,' she warned.

'Let me be the judge of that.'

Sara felt a cold shiver of apprehension as he said this. It's not him I fear most but myself, she thought.

The candlesticks had been a surprise, but the starter Drew presented to her was even more so. She viewed with astonishment the caviare in a white bowl decorated with curls of lemon.

'Sorry there's no ice,' Drew said, handing her a biscuit. 'Clever of me to remember you like caviar, isn't it?'

'I only remember that we ever had it once,' Sara told him, spooning it on to her biscuit.

Cunningly clever of him to remember that particular occasion, their first wedding anniversary when they seemed to have forgotten all their differences and had gone to Windhoek to celebrate. It had been such a luxury to young Sara to leave the wilderness and stay in a luxury hotel and be fed caviar and other delicacies. She had responded to Drew's lovemaking that night with astonishing fervour. It had been wonderful, but that was only one occasion among a host of misunderstandings. He knew that she would remember that night. She was surprised, however, that he himself had remembered it.

'Seafood cocktail next,' said Drew. 'Also out of a tin. I cooled it in the spring. It makes a good refrigerator, as you'll see when you taste this wine.'

There were beautiful glasses with curved stems into which he poured the clear golden wine.

'Are these also the Baron's?' asked Sara. 'How could he have left these beautiful things behind?'

'He left in a hurry, I believe, under threat of war. He took most of his valuables but not such breakable objects as glasses. I suppose he thought they could easily be replaced.'

Sara sipped the beautiful wine. She was beginning to feel more relaxed. There was something very strange and exotic about having this luxurious meal with the golden candelabrum glowing on Drew's dark features and the sounds of the wilderness dulled by the thickness of the walls and the crackling of the logs as they dissolved into flame. The only intruders were the geckos, and she had never minded those. They were small lizards with feet that made them able to stick to the walls, and she had always found their strange little barks a friendly sound.

Drew was setting himself out to be charming, she thought.

'Beware the Greeks bearing gifts,' she said as he came in from the kitchen with a small pheasant surrounded by heated game chips, green peas and baby carrots.

'That could hardly refer to tinned pheasant, surely,' he told her. 'Now if I were to offer you diamonds . . . but I never did, Sara, did I? We were married in such a hurry that you never even had an engagement ring. You reproached me for that once, I remember.'

Do you remember all the bitter words we spoke to each other then? she thought, but she didn't ask him aloud. No use regretting anything. It's all over and done with, and I should never have come to meet him again. Then I wouldn't be sitting near him with the firelight turning his hair to dark russet gold and his eyes tawny as one of those wild creatures out there in the darkness. His eyes. How much can he see now? It seemes to me that his sight has improved a little to how it was when I first came. He managed this dinner very well, and without asking me for help. He seemed determined to do it himself. Perhaps that too was a ploy in aid of my seduction. Oh, Drew, I learned long ago to be impervious to your charm. Or did I?

'What are the long, long thoughts you're having?' he queried. 'Don't I get any praise for my cooking?'

'You planned it very well,' Sara told him.

'Yes, I'm a genius at planning.'

He stretched out his hand and caught hers in a warm steady grasp.

'Life in the wilderness is not so bad after all—confess it, Sara.'

Close at hand penetrating the sounds within, there was the sudden unearthly wailing of a hyena, like the moaning of some spirit come out of the grave. Sara shuddered.

'It's bad enough when you hear noises like that!' she told him.

'The hyena and the jackal aren't so bad as they're painted. They're efficient hunters in their own right, not just the mobile garbage disposal units that's the popular notion of them.'

'It doesn't make that noise any more attractive to me,' Sara assured him as another witchlike cackle shattered the night. It seemed to her that the weird screeching penetrated the thickness of the walls of their retreat, bringing the dark primitive passions of Africa into their pretence at civilisation and making clear the basic fact that here they were, a man and a woman alone in the wilderness and surrounded by the savageries of the animal kingdom.

'I find it attractive,' said Drew. 'There are certain things that one associates with Africa—the roar of the lion welcoming the dawn, the shout of the fish eagle proclaiming himself king of the skies, the shout of the ibis overhead, the quarrelling of monkeys, but to me the jackal and hyena make sounds just as typical. I'd miss those melancholy sounds in the African night.'

'I could do without them right now,' said Sara.

But soon the sounds of ghostly laughter died away and Sara found herself drinking the wine from her refilled glass. Drew had even concocted a sweet served in beautiful cut glass goblets.

'Peaches Cardinal—or an attempt at it,' he announced proudly. They were tinned peach halves, of course, surrounded by a puree of tinned raspberries. 'Don't expect to eat like this every night,' he warned. 'Tomorrow you can produce the meal.'

'I expected as much,' said Sara, laughing. 'I thought all this was too good to be true.'

'It's a celebration of our first day in the wilderness. Our German doctor was right, I hope. Already I'm feeling great, and I haven't even tested the rest of his theory yet.'

He gave her a wicked glance, a look full of sexual attraction.

'I've no wish to participate in a test of his theory,' Sara said primly. 'I've told you before, you should have brought Maxine.'

'Why are you harping on about Maxine? Can't you forget everyone else, Sara? As part of this experiment, I want you to imagine that you and I are the only people in the world. As indeed we are in this world.'

'I'm not interested in your experiment,' she persisted.

'But I am. My lovely Sara, what's happened to you in Paris? You never used to be so cold.'

'I didn't have much sense in those days.'

It was hard to resist the attraction of that mobile mouth, of the hands that had seized hers across the table, of the eyes that seemed to be holding her in their spell. It was as if she were holding on to a dynamo and an electric current was flowing into her blood from those long magnetic fingers.

'I want you, Sara—you know that, don't you? And you want me, however much you may deny it. What difference can it make in your life if you accept that fact now, if we make the most of this short time together? And when we return, as we'll have to some time to normal life, we're quite free to go our separate ways.'

'As if nothing had happened? Oh, no, Drew, you don't get me that way. I don't relish being part of an experiment, however much you may need me for it.'

'It could be a delightful kind of one, you must agree.'

'I don't think so. It wouldn't be delightful to me.'

His smile vanished and his expression darkened.

'I dare you to kiss me and say that again.'

'I can't accept your dare.'

'Because you know you're lying, Sara. You're very tempted—don't deny it. Why are you resisting me? Is there some lover in Paris to whom you have vowed eternal fidelity?'

'Yes, there is. What do you expect after all this time?'

'Your voice has a slight quiver,' he commented. 'What a pity I can't see you properly. I always knew when you were lying because your face flushed a delicious shade of peach. I wonder if it's doing that now?'

'Why should I be lying?' she shrugged.

'Why indeed? But, Sara, if indeed he exists, this French lover is five thousand miles away, and I happen to be right here. If he knows you've spent this time with me, he'll suspect the worst anyway. What difference does it make if we make his suspicions a reality?'

'It makes a difference to me.'

'You mean you won't be able to face him knowing that we've slept together? But, Sara, he knows that we were married. I've possessed you before, so why not now?'

'He didn't know me then. He would feel differently about it now.'

In her mind's eye, Sara summoned up a picture of this fictitious lover, a Frenchman, she had implied. He had better be a Parisian, sophisticated, suave, civilised, the very opposite of this man who sat opposite to her frowning at her with that wild animal glow in the eyes that were dark in the candlelight.

'What's this man like who commands your fidelity?' Drew wanted to know.

'Very good-looking, very well dressed, his hair is a little long, but he goes to a hairdresser frequently. He has his clothes tailored. Sometimes he wears Italian clothes but sometimes he prefers English. He enjoys opera and the theatre and he knows all the best restaurants. He's very ... well, what young girls call "dishy".'

'He sounds quite a guy!' he commented. 'Like something in a TV ad. How would he make out in the wilderness, I wonder?'

'He wouldn't, but then neither would you in his background.'

She wanted to be deliberately cruel; it was the only way to fend him off.

'You might be surprised,' Drew told her.

'Well, you've certainly surprised me tonight with this

meal,' she admitted. 'It's been absolutely delicious, Drew.'

'Glad you liked it—but it isn't finished yet. What do you say to a long leisurely coffee session with liqueurs? Make yourself comfortable on the mattress in front of the fire while I do the necessary.'

Sara sat on the mattress, her face turned to the glowing logs. The lodge with its thick stone walls was beautifully cool in the torrid heat of the day, but at night the fire was necessary when the chills of evening penetrated the cracked windows. I've put him off, she thought, with my talk of a French lover. Even now I can't bear to lie to him, but it was the only thing to do. If I give in to him, he can still twist my heart into little pieces. It's taken three years for me to recover from him. And if I have this short affair with him, recovering from it could take another three. So it isn't going to start.

Drew was soon back with the coffee that smelled as fragrant as only good coffee can. There was brandy in a balloon glass for him and apricot liqueur for her. He had even provided peppermints of a fondant kind that would not melt in the heat.

'As I said before, you think of everything,' Sara told him.

'Oh, I'm wonderful. Can your Frenchman make coffee like this?'

'Of course.'

'Not better?'

'I didn't say so.'

'But you think so. Ah, well, I dare say I could excel him in other more important things.'

That wicked smile was back again.

'Such as?' asked Sara.

'Such as making love, of course. Aren't you the least bit curious to find out whether that's so, Sara? We always hit it off that way, however much we differed in other ways—or does my memory play me false?'

'Perhaps not, but now I'm a different person from the young girl you married, Drew.'

'And even more beautiful.'

'How can you know that?'

'You mean I can't see you properly. Well, Sara, that, I must admit, is frustrating, but I have other means of knowing—Maxine's jealousy, Clive's admiration, and then I can feel it through my fingers—your silky hair, the shape of your face, the curve of your breasts. My fingers are very sensitive. I wonder when I'm going to have the opportunity to find out more about you in this way.'

'You must go on wondering, Drew,' she said firmly.

'I don't remember that you were so hard-hearted in former days. Ah, well, my curiosity may have to go unsatisfied, it seems.'

'Yes, you must resign yourself to that.'

'But I'm not a very resigned character, am I? Even to loss of sight, much less to loss of my wife to some Frenchman.'

'Don't be ridiculous, Drew!' she sighed. 'I'm not your wife any more, and haven't been for three years.'

'Then why did you come back here?'

'You know why I came back. Clive asked me to come, to see if I could be of any help to you.'

'And so you could, if you were willing,' Drew assured her.

'I thought I might help you in practical matters. Your love life is not my affair any more.'

'I had hoped it might be, for a little while anyway. But I see now I'm wrong. Is your response absolutely frigid when I do this, for instance?'

His hand was under her chin and he was turning her face to receive his kiss. His mouth came down on hers, hard and sure. Every nerve in her body was stretched taut as she tried to resist the dizzying ecstasy that invaded all her senses. It was a long, long kiss, and when he had finished he seemed to be looking at her for a long time, searching desperately to see her expression. For once she was glad he could not see her face properly.

'Sorry, Drew, my response is frigid,' she said quietly.

He smiled crookedly.

'You could have fooled me,' he said.

Just at that moment, there was a loud thump on the door, and Sara felt as if she had jumped two feet into the air.

'What on earth was that?' she exclaimed.

But before Drew could reply, they both heard the noise of the lions, deep grunts, vibrating growls, a kind of grumbling conversation going on between them.

'It's the lions come back,' said Sara, trembling with fright.

'Not to worry,' Drew said soothingly. 'All the doors are closed.'

'But are they safe if the lions bang against them like that? Some of those hinges look pretty rusty to me.'

Some more growls and another thump. The door appeared to Sara to quiver, and she wondered how long the old hinges could last if the lions persisted.

'Poor Sara, you're quivering like the leaves on the tamboti tree. Do you want me to scare them off?'

He was holding her in his arms, and this time she did not resist him, because it was comforting just to feel those strong arms around her trying to console her fear.

'Yes—no—I don't know. Please don't leave me, Drew.'

'I'll have to if I'm to scare them away.'

'What are you going to do to them?' she asked.

'Fire a shot into the air. I can do it through the window—that's what they were made for. The place is built like a fort.'

'All right,' she consented as another angry roar sounded outside.

Drew went to fetch his gun and then peered through the slitlike window.

'Good grief, Sara, just come and look! They're magnificent! I've never seen such enormous beasts.'

'I don't think I want to see them,' she shuddered.

'Come along,' he urged. 'You may never have such an opportunity again.'

He seemed to think he was doing her a favour by making a space for her so she could see out of the

window. Gingerly she stood on the box he held out for
her. He had a powerful torch and was shining it
through the narrow slit of the window. She remembered
now that he had said he could see more clearly at night,
but there was no need for keen eyesight to sense the
enormous power of these savage beasts that were only a
few yards away. The moon was rising, silvering the air,
so that sometimes the lion's shadowy forms merged into
the landscape and sometimes they stood out clear-cut as
black paper silhouettes. It was one huge black-maned
male who was still persistently trying to gain admittance
to the lodge.

'I thought you said they did their hunting at night.
Why is this one trying to get into the lodge?' asked
Sara.

'He may be attracted by our smell.'

'But you said that that would scare them off.'

'Not always. Some are more curious than others.
This one may scent the possibility of obtaining a
gourmet dish.' Drew laughed and put his arm around
her. 'Don't look so frightened! I was only teasing.'

'I don't know how you can laugh at a time like this,'
shuddered Sara. 'Aren't you going to do anything
about scaring them off?'

'I should think they'll presently go of their own
accord. After all, they usually like to do their tracking
under a hunter's moon.'

There was another loud thump as the black-maned
lion threw his heavy body against the door.

'Please, Drew, do something,' Sara pleaded. 'Those
bolts aren't going to hold much longer.'

'Oh, very well, he does seem a little too persistent.
Obstinate fellow, he seems to have made up his mind he
wants entrance.'

Drew thrust his gun through the slit of the window
and fired a shot into the air. Sara, holding her hands
over her ears, thought it was worse than the sound of
the lions. The echoes of the shot reverberated through
the empty spaces of the wilderness, seeming to be thrust
back by the rocky cliffs far away. Baboons barked from

their strongholds and birds flew screaming from their roosting places in the tops of trees, but the lions seemed scarcely disturbed. They grumbled to each other as if discussing this extraordinary noise but did not appear to be frightened off by it.

'We'll try something else,' said Drew. 'These lions are going to be a confounded nuisance to us if they insist on hanging around all night.'

'I'm glad you've at last reached that conclusion,' said Sara thankfully.

'Go and fetch me a firebrand,' he ordered. 'You'll be able to choose a suitable one better than I can. There's a pair of tongs there. Mind you carry them carefully.'

The fire was hot, but Sara managed to find a piece of wood that was only partly burned. She took it in the tongs and rather fearfully carried it towards the place where Drew stood at the window.

'Take care. It's burning quickly,' she warned him.

He took hold of the burning brand and with a swing of the wrist, threw it towards the persistent lion. The lion gave a yelp of anger as the sparks flew around it and then, to Sara's infinite relief, it retreated to join its companions. Before it did so, however, it seemed to look towards them, and to Sara it conveyed a deep sense of menace, an aura of absolute power. Soon the lions had gone, silver shadows melting into the blue haze of the moonlit landscape.

'We should have no more trouble now,' said Drew. 'I'm quite sure they intend to hunt tonight. They were just momentarily diverted by their curiosity about us. Nothing surprises me about lions. You know what cats are like, and they're similar in some ways.'

'Those kind of cats are far too large for my liking,' Sara shuddered.

'And now where were we? Ah, yes, you were proving to me that my kisses don't mean anything to you. That was it, wasn't it?'

His crooked smile hurt her heart, and she was determined there was to be no more of his lovemaking that really didn't mean much to him but meant too much to her.

'I've had enough for one day, Drew,' she said firmly. 'I'm going to bed now.'

'You still have ideas of sleeping in the Baron's room?'

'Yes. I found sheets in one of the drawers. It's adequately made up and, it's so hot and dry here it can scarcely not be aired.'

'And I'm not invited there?' asked Drew.

'No definitely not!'

'Take care the Baron's ghost doesn't come to haunt you,' he warned. 'They tell me he was an amorous rogue.'

'I'll risk it,' said Sara.

'It's bound to give you romantic dreams, so if you need me just whistle.'

'I'm too shattered to have dreams, romantic or otherwise. Goodnight, Drew.'

'Only you can give me the good night I desire, Sara, but sleep well.'

She took the lamp that he offered her and made her way up the stone staircase, her shadow long and slender in front of her. When she entered the large hexagonal-shaped room, shadows from the lamp danced in gigantic shapes on the walls and ceiling. Before her bath she had made an attempt at cleaning the room, for she was determined not to spend another night on the mattress in the firelit living room with Drew. But the spiders' webs had defeated her, festooning the central crystal chandelier, as also had the lack of any broom to sweep the floor. However, she had taken off the lace coverlet from the bed and had made it up with the fine linen embroidered sheets that she had found in the carved chest. These at least were clean and, by the light of the lamp, she could see the shadowy recesses of the rest of the room and could ignore the evidence of neglect that was all around her and concentrate on the shabby faded splendour of her surroundings.

The nightdress she had with her was just as good, surely, as any that the Baron's mistresses could have had. It was made of fine black silk chiffon encrusted with pale cream lace and was one of the perquisites she had been given by Madame in an unusually generous

moment at some time when she had been pleased with
her. It had been totally unsuitable for the life in the
camp, but here, she thought, it could come into its own.
If the Baron's ghost was looking on, he could perhaps
appreciate its Parisian elegance.

When she climbed up the steps provided, into the
large fourposter bed with its carvings of cupids and
nymphs, she did not douse the lamp but only lowered it
a little, thinking that possibly she should be careful with
the oil. And she lay looking at her surroundings that
were so incongruously magnificent in the midst of this
savage country. Outside distant hyenas cackled like a
chorus of witches on Walpurgis Night and a distant
elephant trumpeted to its mates, but here all around her
there was this exotic atmosphere.

Above the bed in the ceiling there was a mirror, faded
now, but surrounded with swags of gold. Crumbling
tapestries on the walls depicted classic scenes of gods
and goddesses, leading what looked like a most
unrestrained love life. Just as well I can't see them too
clearly, Sara thought. Her eyes were feeling heavy now,
and with a last glimpse of herself lying in the very
centre of the bed, black chiffon dark against the
whiteness of the sheets and red-gold hair loosened and
flowing over the lace pillow, she went to sleep.

She had a feeling that she had been asleep for some
hours when something woke her. Could it have been an
especially loud noise from outside in the wilderness?
But no, strangely enough at this time the sounds of the
savage outside world had stilled and there was a
menacing kind of silence, a quiet that Sara expected to
be broken by some fearful noise at any moment.

All at once she realised with horror that it was in this
room, and it wasn't anything very loud, just a stealthy
sort of rustling that seemed to be coming from directly
beneath her. And then there was a kind of slithering
noise, not like the padding steps of an animal with paws
but a puzzling sound, soft and slippery. She sat by now
completely awake and thoroughly alarmed. What on
earth could it be?

Sitting bolt upright in bed, she turned up the lamp from its previous gentle glow, and then she saw it, and at the same time, with a vicious flick of its tail, it turned and saw her. It was a creature that could have come from some prehistoric time, a giant lizard like a small dragon but at least five feet long. Regarding her with cold evil green eyes, it puffed itself up to its full size, hissing and flicking its great forked tongue. Its shining dark scales glittered like armour in the lamplight and its malevolent gaze was fixed on Sara as if it were trying to hypnotise her.

'Drew!' she screamed. 'Can you hear me? Come here quickly, and bring your gun!'

Her screams did not seem to scare the monster, rather they seemed to enrage it more, and it stood its ground heaving itself up and down and puffing and hissing at her. Sara tried to make herself as small as possible in the vast bed, hoping that it was not capable of climbing up by the set of steps beside it.

'Drew,' she screamed again, 'please come here!'

The door burst open and he stood there clad only in a pair of short pants, his hair ruffled by sleep, holding the gun in his hand.

'For God's sake, Sara, what is it?'

The noise of the door had alarmed the lizard and it had retreated into a corner of the room. She gestured to it, too frightened to speak. At last she found her voice.

'It's a huge kind of lizard. It must have been under my bed all the time. Can you see it, Drew? Oh, what are we to do? It looks so fierce and violent. Can you see it at all?'

'I can see it's outline.'

'Then shoot it. Shoot it quickly, or else give me the gun if you can't see it well enough for that. Otherwise it's going to do us both harm!'

'My poor Sara, you've obviously become very unaccustomed to the bush, that's quite evident. Surely you know these things are quite harmless? They make a great thing of showing their aggression, lashing their tails, hissing and so on, but they're quite incapable of fighting. Poor creature, you've probably scared it half to death with that screaming. I thought at least a python had invaded your room!'

Drew strode across to the corner where the creature was hissing and grunting, and taking it firmly by the neck and the tail, so that it was incapacitated, he marched with it to the door.

'I'll be back,' he promised her.

She was trembling all over and she tried her best to stop, but it only seemed to make it worse. How could she have been expected to know that the fierce pre-historic-looking creature was harmless? It had looked tremendously powerful with its strong tail and ugly head. Another mark against her from Drew, she supposed. Maxine would have known it was harmless. She would have probably sprung out of bed and taken a photograph of it. Sara had been determined to put a brave face on things, but when Drew came back into the room she felt so unnerved that she burst into tears.

'My poor Sara,' he said, sitting on the bed and taking her into his arms.

'I'm not your poor Sara,' she snapped. 'But I didn't expect the company of giant lizards in the Baron's bedroom.'

'You can expect anything in this place,' he told her.

'So it seems!' Sara shuddered.

'Now you can see how unwise it was of you to decide to sleep alone. You'd better let me stay to protect you against any other nocturnal visitors.' His expression was one of wicked charm and his mouth was very near to hers. 'It seems I'm between the devil and the deep blue sea,' she sighed.

'Then choose the devil,' he told her.

When he slid the lacy straps of her nightdress from her shoulders and kissed the curves of her breasts, Sara knew she had lost. He had brought back the wild desires of her youth, and, as he pushed her back upon the bed and bent over her, she could see their reflection in the Baron's mirror, two figures like the lovers on the tapestries, utterly absorbed in each other and the fulfilment of their passion.

CHAPTER ELEVEN

Now Sara was prepared to believe Drew when he had said for a short time they could live in paradise. She had surrendered herself to him so completely that now there could be no going back. They were two people in a world of their own, a place in which the outside world had no part, and yet she knew it was the outside world that was real and her present life was like a dream, or one of those mirages over the dry water of the pan that vanished when one came too near.

And with Drew as her lover beside her, the wilderness was losing some of its terrors. She was learning to know it and not be so afraid. She wanted to ask him, 'Why didn't we ever do this before?' but she did not want to remind him of that former life when he had excluded her from this part of his life. I guess I was too immature, she thought. I didn't have the wisdom to cope with a man like Drew. But have I the wisdom now? It scarcely matters, does it? When we have to return, this will all be over; he made that quite clear in the beginning when he suggested a short affair. She tried to put this thought behind her and live for the present.

It seemed to her too that during the last few days his eyesight had definitely improved, but she was afraid to ask if this was so, but when they were out on their walks into the wilderness, he seemed to notice more, and she was convinced this couldn't only be because of his hearing and sense of smell. Was she being too hopeful? But that German doctor had assured her that with rest and relaxation it might improve. A second honeymoon, Drew had suggested. Well, in spite of her opposition to the idea it had happened. I must just make up my mind, she thought, to have no regrets when this is over, as it will be very soon. But how will I be able to help it? Just don't think of it now.

'What I would really like to do,' Drew said when they had been there a few days, 'would be to take a tent and a sleeping bag and spend a few days away from here. We're too highly civilised here, sleeping in the Baron's bed. Let's get away from it all. What do you say? Do you think you're up to it?'

'I suppose I can try,' Sara told him.

Secretly she was horrified at the idea. Wandering in the wilderness was full of surprises, some not always pleasant, but having to face night-time with no stone walls to protect them sounded truly terrifying to her, but she dared not, indeed she could not refuse him anything in this present state of dreaming passion.

She would never have thought she could regret leaving the lodge, but now, looking back at it as they went over the hill, it seemed like home to her. And in front of them lay the wilderness, with goodness knows how many shocks in store.

'The days warm early here. We'll get our walking done before noon,' said Drew. 'I aim to get to a place I know that had a waterhole with a windpump. We'll get clear water there, but the animals know it too and we'll see plenty of life around it.'

'Will there be lions?' asked Sara.

'I hope so, and elephants too if we're lucky.'

Let's hope we're unlucky, thought Sara, but she dared not spoil his enthusiasm by saying this aloud.

'It's getting on now to the hottest time of the year,' Drew added.

'And the dustiest,' Sara agreed as she toiled through the sandy soil of a river bed. The shade of the thorn trees was very welcome, and now and then they saw animals that were appreciating this too. A group of zebras flashed through the trees, looking with their striped coats like something from a circus.

'Did you know,' Drew informed her, 'that zebras can stay faithful to their mates for a lifetime, say fifteen or twenty years?'

'That's easy when they have so many wives,' said Sara. 'What you really mean is it's the wives that stay faithful.'

'You could be right. What a pity you aren't a zebra, Sara.'

'So that you could enjoy my faithfulness while disporting yourself with younger females? No, thank you, Drew. I prefer to be what I am.'

'Unfaithful to your French lover?'

'Let's forget about him for now,' said Sara.

'Willingly. I was only wondering whether you're suffering any pangs of conscience.'

'That's my affair,' she shrugged.

'Will you tell him about us?'

'I hardly think so. Will you tell Maxine?'

'Maxine can draw her own conclusions,' said Drew enigmatically.

'When I get back to Paris, this will all seem like a dream,' Sara sighed.

'Then we'll go on dreaming for a little while longer, shall we?'

He put his arm around her waist and she turned her face to be kissed. The slow languorous kiss was in harmony with the sultry heat of the day and the hot fragrance of wild grass underneath the burning sun. She told herself fiercely not to look beyond this desperate enchantment of the senses that now held her in thrall, but a part of her seemed to stand aside and feel weak with despair at the idea of parting from him again.

'One of these days we will have to make plans for getting back,' Drew said, as if reading her thoughts. 'At this time of year, there should be a possibility of rain. It doesn't always come, but if it does the roads become well-nigh impassable.'

'How can you tell when rain is coming?' she asked.

'Various signs—clouds and lightning on the horizon, worse dust devils than usual. We'll know soon enough if we're going to get rain. But it mostly hangs back. Some places haven't had rain for seven years.'

'But how are we to get back if the car won't start?'

Drew smiled enigmatically.

'We'll think of something.'

It was then that Sara had a fleeting suspicion of the

truth, but she did not care to pursue it. I'm too happy, she thought, to mistrust him. Let everything happen as he wills it. We'll have to go back into the real world soon enough.

'Just look at those ground squirrels!' she exclaimed. 'Whatever are they doing?'

'They're spreading their tails to shelter themselves from the heat. They use their tails as a sort of portable sunshade after scraping loose sand over themselves.'

'Very clever of them to think of that.'

'It seems to be instinctive in most animals to find ways to protect themselves against extreme heat,' Drew told her. 'Wildebeest plaster themselves with mud as do elephants too. Jackals lie down in any bit of mud they can find and warthogs wallow in it. But I must say that mud gets scarcer and scarcer at this time of year. However, we'll find the spring we're heading for is not dried up because there's a pump there. So we'll be all right.'

It was not so much the lack of water that Sara dreaded but the close proximity of animals during the night hours, but she could not fight against Drew's determination to spend the night out in the wilderness. In the late afternoon, they arrived at the place where Drew had decided to camp. It was a beautiful glade in the midst of the variegated leaves of the mopane trees.

'We'll stay near enough to the spring to be able to carry water but not so near as to disturb the animals coming to it,' Drew told her.

'That's a relief,' said Sara. 'It's me they'll disturb.'

'I thought you were getting used to life in the bush.'

'Not to spending the night here!'

'Stop fretting,' soothed Drew. 'It's going to be the most wonderful night of your life.'

'I'm glad you think so. I'm not so sure.'

'Why are you so timid?' he asked. 'Maxine would give anything to spend a night out in the wilderness. Unfortunately she was forbidden to do that. The authorities thought it might be too dangerous for her, and for once she listened to them.'

'You surprise me,' said Sara coldly. 'Are you sorry now that you didn't bring Maxine with you?'

He turned to her with that lively wicked smile. 'What do you think?'

I don't know what to think, she thought to herself. I don't know how much you're involved with Maxine. You grasped your opportunity with me because I was here and because in the end I couldn't resist your lovemaking, but you made it quite plain that it was only for the duration of our stay. You're using me for just a little while, but when we get back to the camp, you'll expct me to go back to Paris as if nothing had happened.

'We must gather a good supply of wood before the sun goes down,' Drew told her now. 'We'll need to keep the fire going all night. And before it gets dark we'll go to the waterhole. There should be plenty for you to see there.'

The glowing light of the lowering sun now turned the water of the pool to molten gold as Drew and Sara approached the waterhole. They came there quietly, and Drew indicated a bush behind which they could remain unseen and yet see the pool. First the zebras came, kicking rudely at a group of wildebeest who were in their way. They were very boisterous and jolly, sometimes rolling round in the wet sand and behaving like the clowns that they appeared to be. Then the springbok, more timid, keeping a wary eye around them and dashing away for cover at the slightest suspicious movement. A kudu made its stately way down to the water's edge with stiff, dignified gait and large curling horns. Warthogs came in family parties, running towards the water with tails straight up in the air, often wallowing in the mud, rolling and twisting with joy at being cool at last. A troop of baboons arrived and stayed drinking for a long time. One youngster fell in and had to be rescued by an anxious mother, dripping and scared. Some of the young baboons pestered the adults so much that they got soundly spanked and their anguished screams and yells echoed through the trees. But suddenly all signs of life vanished.

'What is it?' whispered Sara.

'Look to your left.'

A family of lions were processing towards the pool as if they owned the world.

'They usually drink before the night's hunting,' Drew whispered.

A large male and three females crouched down at the water's edge. The sound of their lapping tongues came clearly across the pool. The four cubs with them were in a more playful mood, however; they were not interested in drinking but teased the adults just as the baboons had done before. Two of them played with the lion's tail, nipping it with their sharp teeth so that at last he turned around and gave a low growl. They did the same to one of the lionesses, and Sara was astonished at how gently she chastised them when they had evidently hurt her. All that happened was that she gave them a gentle cuff that sent them sprawling on the wet sand. Then she went back to her drinking.

Sara described it all to Drew in an excited whisper. She was not sure how much he could see, but he seemed to be managing quite well.

'I told you before,' he whispered, 'lions are a friendly lot with each other. They're great family beasts. They have a way of bonding, touching each other in a kind of caress, that seems to create affection. And of course they're the only animals that get together in a proper plan of attack when hunting.'

'I never knew they were so fascinating,' said Sara. 'I've always been too frightened to find out.'

She watched as one of the lionesses picked up the tiniest cub in its mouth, carefully holding it with its great incisors clearly visible and yet it was in the gentlest possible way.

'That's wonderful,' she told Drew. 'I'll never forget seeing them like this.'

'You probably didn't realise that the lions are in the same boat as me sometimes. In diffused light, their vision is impaired so that they see the world in shades of grey. For instance, the stripes of a zebra can appear as a bundle of sticks to them.'

One of the lionesses now started off away from the waterhole and the others followed in single file, the cubs trailing behind them and the great male plodding along in the rear. Soon they vanished into the bush, and the silence that had heralded their coming was broken by the call of the guineafowl flying in for water. Now two giraffes arrived, languorously entwining their necks together in strange gestures of affection, and tiny dik-dik came to drink, glancing nervously around with their huge dark eyes.

'Time to go,' said Drew. 'We must light the fire before the sun goes down.'

As the round red ball of the sun sank below the skyline, the presence of a fire seemed reassuring to Sara. Somewhere out there in the gathering dusk, a lone lion roared, seeming to echo down the empty spaces of the night. As the sun set, it filled the sky with glowing coals of light, turning the sand to red and casting great streamers of flame across the heavens.

'A stormy sunset and clouds on the horizon. One of these days it seems we might get rain, and soon it will be time to go.'

We can't go yet when we've only just found each other, Sara thought, but she did not want to let him know how much these last few days had meant to her. She tried not to think of it as she busied herself heating the stew from a tin. After sunset the sharp cries of the barking geckos echoed from the rocks around them, small bats swooped overhead and somewhere nearby there was a snuffling, rasping noise.

'What's that?' cried Sara, alarmed again.

'Only a porcupine rasping at the bark of a tree. He won't come anywhere near to us, you can be sure of that.'

Somewhere in the bush, a nightjar gave its distinctive call.

'My nanny used to tell me it said, "Good Lord, deliver us,"' said Sara.

'And so it does. Come on, Sara, let's look at the stars.'

He put his arm around her and led her into the clearing. Overhead the stars wheeled and danced in a great universe of light, million upon million, stretching into the outermost limits of space. Sara shuddered, imagining the two of them, tiny figures set in the wilderness with all the heavens above them.

'What's wrong?' asked Drew, feeling her tremble.

'It makes me feel how small we are, here on the edge of this immensity.'

'No need. At this moment we're the most precious two people in the wilderness. Don't you know, don't you feel, Sara, that paradise is all around us? Our heaven is now.' He lifted her up and carried her into the tent. 'No time for being morbid about how small we seem underneath the sky,' he said, smiling down at her. 'I'm going to show you how important we are. I intend to make love to you as you've never been made love to before.'

Sara was glad this night that he undressed her without haste, kissing her with slow sensuous passion between the discarding of each garment.

'We have all the time in the world,' he told her. 'All the time in the universe.'

But presently his lovemaking was like a flame pulsating through her body. Feverishly she returned his kisses, feeling at the last that she was drowning in throbbing waves of desire. She felt he was taking her away into some country that was far stranger, far more heavenly even than this wilderness in which they had found each other.

But when at last he slept, cradled on her shoulder, she lay awake a long time, hearing the nightjar shout his melancholy cry, seeing through the opening of the tent the great bowl of the heavens with its myriad shining stars. Then she felt the tears start in her eyes and run slowly down her cheeks. How am I going to be able to forget him? she asked. How am I going to be able to bear it when we're parted by thousands of miles again?

She got up to put more wood on the fire, and found

to her surprise that she was not frightened any more of the darkness, nor of the distant cough of a leopard followed closely by the screams of a baboon. I must be getting used to it, she thought. Low on the horizon she could see flashes of lightning and a rumble of thunder sounded faint and far away, and now with the prospect of rain and being forced to get back to camp she felt nothing but dread.

She awoke to the cool light of dawn and Drew was up before her, kindling the fire into a blaze in the blue of the morning with the welcome fragrance of coffee and in the air the calling of many birds. Walking across the clearing, Sara felt completely refreshed with such a feeling of wellbeing she could have laughed aloud. They breakfasted hugely on fried smoky-tasting bacon and scrambled eggs.

'I could stay here for ever,' she told Drew.

She had not mentioned the fact that she had noticed the lightning and thunder, but Drew had seen it too.

'Sorry, my dear one,' he said, 'but we'd better get back to the lodge. There are all the signs of rain, and if we get stuck here by floods we may have difficulty in getting out.'

She had a sinking feeling. This then was the beginning of the end.

'Must we really?' she protested. 'But I don't understand how you expect we can get out anyway with the car out of action. Will we have to walk to the main road?'

'Oh, that. My sweet Sara, you didn't really believe there was anything vitally wrong with the car, did you?'

'But it won't go. We both tried to start it. You said it was the coil.'

'You suggested it might be the coil and I accepted your explanation. No, Sara, I must confess it—I took the rotor arm out.'

'You *what*?' she gasped.

'Very simple. It's just a little thing, the size of my thumb, that fits on to the centre shaft of the distributor. Without it the engine won't start. All I have to do is to put it back and then we can escape the rain.'

Sara was suddenly so angry that for a moment she could not speak.

'Do you mean to say that we could have gone back at any time?' she demanded then.

'Of course.'

He was smiling, and she wanted to hit the smug expression from his face.

'But why—why did you do it?'

'I had to do something desperate. You seemed so determined to go and leave me. I couldn't let you go upsetting my plans, now could I?'

'I think you're completely unscrupulous and incorrigible!' she snapped furiously. 'How could you have kept me here against my will by telling me such lies?'

'It hasn't been against your will the last few days, has it?' he grinned.

'You did this all on purpose! It hurt your vanity that I kept refusing to be made love to, and you kept me here knowing that . . . oh, I could kill you!'

'I knew that eventually you would sensibly come to the conclusion that we had something going for us if only for a little while—and it worked, didn't it, Sara? You can't say you haven't enjoyed the last few days, can you?'

'I hate you! You deliberately deceived me in the lowest possible way.'

'Of course I did. A fellow has to be pretty desperate to be forced to resort to such means to seduce his own wife. Anything's fair in love and war, you should know that.'

'I don't know it. I don't want to discuss it even. All I want to do is to get back to the lodge and go back to the camp. And as soon as I get back there I'm leaving. I don't care if I never see you again!' she finished.

'You always were a damned unreasonable woman, Sara,' sighed Drew. 'I don't understand why you're so angry. After all, it takes two to live as we've done during the last few days. It was hardly rape, now was it?'

'It was worse than that. I don't want to talk about it

any more. But take it from me, Drew, tonight you can sleep alone, tonight and every night.'

It was worse than rape, she had told him. It was worse because he had deliberately set out to charm her and had kept her here knowing that, if he did not let her go, in a few days she would succumb to his charm. Of course she had known all along that it could not last, but she did not know it had all been deliberate on his part. She would much rather have thought that they were both overwhelmed by the same passion rather than that he had deliberately planned her seduction.

'At least admit, Sara, that the last days have meant quite a lot to you, that you've begun to see the wilderness in a different light,' he pursued.

'That's nonsense. You know I've always hated it, and now I hate it more than ever.'

But that wasn't true, Sara knew. She just wanted to get back at Drew for his deception. During the last few days she had learned to love the wilderness, this strange background for her passion for Drew. But now she was not going to admit it. The short affair was over, and so was her attraction to the wilderness.

As they made their way back to the lodge, it was obvious that the weather was changing. Heavy black clouds were gathering on the horizon and there were fitful fierce gusts of wind with spinning dust devils that brought stinging sand into the eyes.

'We'll start off at early light tomorrow. We wouldn't be able to get there today before dark,' Drew promised.

True to her word, Sara slept alone, a restless, troubled sleep. During the night she awoke to hear the sound of rain thrown against the window by the gusts of wind. Sheets of lightning lit up the dark velvet sky and thunder moaned from a long way off. It was hot and humid and uncomfortable, and she lay on top of the sheets in the Baron's bed, trying not to think of the other nights she had spent here.

Towards morning she woke from a troubled sleep to hear what sounded like a deluge pouring down on the parched earth. Soon afterwards she heard Drew's footsteps on the stairs and then his voice calling to her. It was difficult to make out his words for the sound of rain hammering upon the roof of the lodge, and she got up and opened the door. He was wearing only a pair of brief shorts and he was wet as a seal, the hair on the bronzed muscles of his chest dripping with raindrops and his hair plastered to his brow in sculptured curls.

'Get dressed and packed straight away, Sara,' he told her. 'We must get going. Once this starts it's liable to continue. We can expect the rivers to flood at any time.'

Sara laughed incredulously.

'What rivers, Drew? Surely not those dry river beds in which we walked?'

'Those dry river beds, Sara, can turn to raging torrents in a matter of hours. I've packed the car as best I could. We can leave the non-essentials here. The tinned food can stay in the cupboards. We'll leave provision for other lovers, shall we?'

Other lovers? As she packed her case hurriedly, Sara realised that she would never again see this place where she had know such shortlived happiness. But it was all over now. Drew was so desperately anxious to get back and be rid of her and resume his normal life that he was using the rains as an excuse to depart. But then she remembered that she herself had wanted to go today, rains or no, and her fury returned at the idea that he had deceived her about the car and had used her while they were here. So she was not in a good mood as they hastily finished packing the car, and the rain pouring all round her and dripping down her neck and making her shirt stick to her skin did nothing to relieve her feelings of anger and frustration.

'Leave the rest and get into the car, Sara. We must get on. Why are you taking so long?'

'I'm being as quick as I can. There's no need to shout at me!' she retorted crossly.

'You don't want to get stuck here, do you?'

'I've been stuck here for too long already, and it was all your doing.'

'I had an idea you'd begun to enjoy it,' he drawled.

'Then you were wrong. You of all people should have known that I could never tolerate this kind of life.'

'You made quite a good pretence of it, then. I could almost have recommended you as a wilderness wife. What's wrong? Have you had second thoughts now about being unfaithful to your French suitor?'

'Not at all. We're all adult people. You can't imagine, Drew, that all this has really meant anything to me? You seem to think you've been using me, but two can play at that game. How do you know I haven't been using you too?'

Just think that one over, Sara thought to herself. He had hurt her pride by the fact that he had seduced her so easily, and she wanted to lash out at him, to wound him as much as he had wounded her.

'I've no time to argue with you now. Sara, Get into the car and let's go.'

'I'd better drive, hadn't I?' she said.

'Not at all. I'm more used to these conditions than you are, and my eyesight isn't as bad as it was. I seem to be able to see more. I wonder now what could have effected the improvement? Could it have been that we followed Dr Buchner's remedy?'

Sara would have dearly loved to do something outrageous, something that would have wiped that wicked smile from his face, but instead she took her seat beside him and prepared to face the hazardous journey back to camp.

It was quite astonishing how the whole landscape had changed with the coming of rain. In a few short hours a lake seemed to have taken the place of the desert. And, where the rain had fallen, the warm sun shining now was bringing open the flowers, pink and white amaryllis, bright yellow tribulus weed that was spreading over the previously dry earth. Blue mist lay over the plains and game tracks had been turned into twisting paths of water. As the earth steamed in the awakening rays of the sun, tortoises were suddenly on the move and the usually dignified-looking gemsbok were leaping and gambolling like young calves. In some of the small pools along the way, they could even hear the croaking of frogs.

But the journey was difficult. The car swerved from side to side on the wet road, skidding deep into the churned mud.

'Won't you let me drive?' Sara asked anxiously as the car skidded from side to side.

'Certainly not. I know this road. I could drive it blindfold, as you probably think I'm doing now. But stop worrying, Sara. My sight is better now than you think.'

Was he being too self-confident? she wondered as they bounced over the rough track, but she could not force him out of the driver's seat.

When they had passed through here before during the day the place had seemed quiet and empty of life, but now with the advent of rain everything seemed to be on the move. Sara saw a lion shaking the water from its wet mane, and as termites, flying ants, rose in fluttering hordes released from their dark homes in the ground, lizards and mongooses darted out to catch them as they fell to the ground after discarding their wings. The lizards sat on the rocks, wings sticking out of their mouths, gorged with the feast.

'Soon the birds will arrive,' said Drew. 'This is a great migration route. All kinds of water birds stay here for a short while—ducks, geese, teal, waders.'

'But how do they know to come here when before this it has been so dry?'

'God knows,' said Drew. 'Quite literally, only God and the ducks know.'

Sara had been enjoying the changed landscape in spite of the rocking and swaying of the vehicle, but now she noticed that black clouds were gathering overhead. The humidity had risen and, all at once, it seemed very warm and oppressive. Over the distant plains, dust devils whirled and danced like live things and quite frequently the heavens seemed to split open with forks of lightning flashing across the bruised looking sky.

'We're in for more rain,' Drew muttered, and he

pressed his foot harder down on the accelerator while the car, leaping forward, skidded and bucketed on the rough road. The rain came down hard with great coin-shaped drops making damp holes in the newly dried dust. It battered against the windscreen, sweeping down in a torrent so that they could not see more than a few feet ahead. Drew had to slow down.

'Let's stop for a while,' Sara pleaded.

'Very well. I don't expect this will last for long.'

But to Sara it seemed to be going on and on. Sitting in the close confinement of the car with the rain battering against it on all sides, they seemed again to be the only persons left alive in the world. Outside she could see across the waterlogged plain, herds of animals, wildebeest, zebras and springbok, standing hunched against the rain, facing away from the downpour. Two male ostriches picked their way with dignity over the flooded road, their splendid black and white plumage waving bedraggled in the breeze.

Sara glanced at Drew. He was sitting quite relaxed as if he had not a care in the world. He doesn't mind, she thought, that when we get back to camp we intend to part for ever. This is all a joke to him, a way of testing his power over me. In the small warm confines of the vehicle, enclosed as they were in this private world, she had a desperate desire to turn to him, to be enclosed in his arms once more, to feel again the passion of his kisses. There was a little pulse beating there in the hollow of his throat just above the place where the silky hairs escaped from his open safari jacket. If I could put my lips on it, she thought, then we would be back where we started. Stop having such idiotic ideas, Sara! she scolded herself. It's all over for both of us. You knew all along that there was no future in it.

'The rain's easing. We'll have another try,' said Drew.

'Are you sure you wouldn't like me to drive? Isn't it rather a strain for you?'

'Look, Sara, the whole landscape is in tones of grey, isn't it? And it's difficult to see through the rain anyway. I don't know that you could manage any better than I, but if you want to have a go, well and good. We haven't got much further to go.'

As they changed seats, Sara thought that at least it would occupy all her thoughts having to drive in these conditions. This way she could not brood about Drew. But it was more difficult than she had realised. Possibly because of the extra rain, the car seemed to slither and slide upon the road much worse than it did before when Drew had been driving.

'Would you like me to drive again?' asked Drew, but she shook her head, determined not to let him see how alarming she was finding it. She had thought that the rain was easing, but it started up again as she struggled on, and it was difficult to tell whether she was driving on the roadway or on the open veld. The road was so rough that she thought she might just as well be driving over the rugged countryside that was on each side of the track.

'Slow down,' said Drew suddenly. 'There's a watercourse somewhere near here, and it will need skill to negotiate it. You'd better let me take over.'

'There's no need,' she told him, suddenly seeing that the road fell away to a steep slope at that point. And just at that moment she felt the car's wheels slide from under her and leap completely out of control. She tried desperately to correct the skid, but the car seemed to have developed a life of its own. It turned around twice in the wet road, landed where it had started, then careered down the slope and was suddenly engulfed by great waves of water. For a few terrifying moments Sara felt the car floating like a submarine, and then it sank. Water was all around, blinding her, and the sudden panic made her unable to think. She felt the car heel over on its side and she was trapped with Drew's heavy weight on top of her.

'Get out of the way,' he said sharply. 'I must open the door. The water may come down stronger at any moment, and then the car could be swept away.'

She felt the heavy weight lift from her as Drew

dragged himself upwards, then he was sitting on the overturned car, and turning to lift her out too.

'Come on, we'll have to swim for it,' he told her, and supporting her against the strong flow of the current, he propelled her towards the farther bank. The stream was not wide, but the drag of the water was very powerful and it was with difficulty that Drew managed to get them to the edge. Then he made her walk up the steep slope on the other side, not letting her rest. Her lungs felt fit to burst as he forced her to get herself up to higher ground.

'I can't do it, Drew!' she panted. 'Please let me stop for a moment.'

'You can do it. Do you want to drown?'

'I feel half drowned already,' Sara gasped, choking over the amount of water she had swallowed.

'One good thing, there aren't any crocodiles here,' she said.

'There were a few snakes, however,' said Drew.

'Now you tell me?' she gasped.

'If I'd said anything before you might not have ventured across the water.'

'Or maybe I'd have gone quicker.'

'Now you can sit a while,' he told her.

She sat on the wet ground at the side of the road. They were both so thoroughly drenched that a little mud didn't seem to make any difference. Sara looked back to where the brown waves swirled and eddied, below them in the place that only yesterday had been a dry river bed. And as they watched, the car heeled over even further and disappeared in the flood.

'There go all those exquisite Paris clothes,' said Drew.

'You don't sound very sorry about it,' she commented wryly.

'I wasn't so sold on them. They were too sophisticated for my simple tastes.'

'I suppose you like your women to be constantly in a safari suit?'

'Not always,' he said, the wicked smile returning.

'Anyway, I have my passport and papers in a waterproof case in my inside pocket,' she told him.

'So you'll still be able to get away quickly. That should make you happy.'

'It does, but what concerns me is what's to happen right now? How do we get back to the camp if we have no transport?'

'We'll have to walk.'

'Is it far?' she asked.

'Not too far. You should be in good training after all the walking we've done lately.'

'I guess there's nothing else for it,' Sara said.

She felt bruised and wet and in no condition for walking, but she was determined she would not show any weakness. Possibly the accident had been her fault, and yet Drew had not reproached her for it. A skein of geese flew overhead uttering their wild weird cries.

'The first migrants,' said Drew. 'They've come from Europe. Don't you wish you could fly there as easily?'

'I wish I could fly right now,' she said.

'Poor Sara! For someone who says she hates the wilderness, you're getting plenty of experience of it. Don't worry, though. I promise you that by tomorrow or the next day, you'll be out of it, and then next stop Paris.'

I should be happy with that idea, thought Sara, but am I?

CHAPTER TWELVE

AFTER it all, had not been as bad as Sara had expected. When they had walked for some way and come to the main road, but were still many miles from the camp, a truck came towards them from the other direction. It was Clive, with a few African guards.

'What the hell are you doing here?' he demanded. 'We thought you were in Johannesburg.'

'We should have been,' said Sara wearily, 'but Drew had other ideas.'

'You look all in,' said Clive. 'What's happened to the car?'

'It's somewhere down one of the spruits,' Drew told him. 'We may be able to retrieve it later. Just get us back to camp, Clive. We'll explain things later.'

'I drove the car into the river. Drew hauled us out,' Sara explained.

'Hard cheese,' was Clive's only comment.

Sara was glad that he didn't press them for any explanation. It was going to be difficult enough to face Maxine and Brad, now that this wild adventure had ended so disastrously. Well, I'll be gone tomorrow or the next day, she thought, and I need never see anyone connected with the wilderness again. The thought of never seeing Drew again made her feel odd. No, that was stupid. She must be suffering from shock; that was why she had this numb feeling about parting from him once more. She must try to forget him all over again.

In a kind of dazed dream she managed to survive the surprise and questioning when they arrived back at the camp. Fortunately Brad was away and she did not have to face him. But Maxine was there, looking more beautiful than ever. She took hold of Drew in a long embrace—far longer than was necessary, Sara thought.

'But how could you have let Drew take such risks?'

she demanded, turning to Sara. 'And you said you were taking him to Johannesburg. All this time I've been thinking he's being cared for and having some kind of medical treatment, and you persuaded him to go on this crazy jaunt!'

Sara did not even bother to deny that it had been her idea. What was the use? she thought. Soon she would be far away from all of them and she would never again have to endure seeing Maxine wind those snakelike arms around Drew's body in that possessive manner.

'Not to worry, Maxine,' said Drew. 'The rest seems to have done something for me. I still see everything in black and grey like a photographic negative, but it seems distinctly clearer than it was.'

'Oh, wonderful! Now you can come and direct my expeditions. That's what I've always wanted. With my photography and your experience of animals, we should be able to get some wizard pictures.'

Not so fast, thought Sara. Drew may be able to see a little better, but he isn't by any means cured. But Drew seemed enthusiastic as he said, 'That sounds great. Now that the rains have come, there'll be a completely different aspect of Etosha that you can photograph. By tomorrow there'll be birds of all kinds around the water places and there'll be a background of new leaves and flowers for you.'

'Then let's go. Let's go as soon as we can. Do you think you'll be fit enough for tomorrow?'

'Certainly. There's nothing wrong with me that another trip into the wilderness won't cure.'

He was smiling at Maxine in the same way he had so often smiled at her, Sara. Oh, Drew, how can you? she thought. We've only just returned, and you've obviously discarded any thought of what happened at the hunting lodge as if it had never been.

'I must go and bath,' she said, and turned away, but Drew did not seem to hear her. He was still talking to Maxine as they arranged the details of tomorrow's trip into the watery wilderness.

*   *   *

That night in the same little chalet on the edge of the camp, Sara slept soundly through sheer exhaustion. She had not seen Drew at all since she had left him with Maxine. After her bath, there had been a discreet knock at her door. A cook brought in a tray of food, soup, an omelette, a glass of wine and coffee. Someone, either Drew or Clive, must have suggested this. Or was it Maxine, she wondered, Maxine wanting Drew's company to herself? Sara had spoken to Clive and they had decided that he would drive her tomorrow to a point where she could get a coach to Windhoek. After seeing Maxine and Drew together, she had decided she must get away as soon as possible. She told herself this ache in her heart must stop paining once she had returned to Paris and taken up her old life.

She awoke some time in the night and listened to the sounds of the wilderness. To her it no longer sounded unfathomable and sinister as it had before. She heard the odd high-pitched call of a zebra disturbed in its sleep and the mournful distant howl of a lonely jackal baying to the moon. Nearby frogs and crickets kept up a continual chorus. Then suddenly there came the sound of a lion's hunting call echoing wild and free across the plains. It paused and everything was silent. Then again the voice of the lion filled the night with sound. Sara found that she was no longer scared. There was something so truly thrilling and magnificent about the lion. She had seen them in a domestic setting, touching each other, playing gently with the cubs. But at night, when their roaring silenced all other creatures in the wilderness, they seemed to her to be truly kings of their savage country. I know now how Drew feels, she thought. I've learned to love it here, but it's all come too late. It should have happened long ago.

She slept again, and this time she did not wake until nine o'clock. The same man who had brought her supper knocked at the door and brought her a tray of breakfast.

'You slept well?' he asked, as she struggled to wake properly.

'I did indeed,' she told him.

'Drew's been up for hours. He went out when the sun came up.'

So he had gone with Maxine as he had planned.

When she had showered and dressed Sara went in search of Clive. She must arrange with him when she could get away. She felt wildly angry with Drew. He had deceived her and used her in the cruellest possible way, and yet she found she was still attracted to him. How could she help it after all that had passed between them? But men were different. He had taken her, seduced her even just because she was there, and now, as soon as they had returned, he had gone back to Maxine.

'Is it true,' she asked Clive, 'that Drew has gone out already with Maxine?'

'Afraid so. She insisted that he must direct her to the best places for photographing the floods and the birds that are coming in, but he left you this note.'

'Very good of him,' said Sara sarcastically.

She opened it with trembling fingers.

'Sara,' she read, 'Clive says he's taking you to catch the coach, so it seems you no longer need me. After all that has happened between us, I think it best not to say goodbye, so I'm going with Maxine to direct her route. Forget the last few days. It was obviously all a mistake, though I can't say I'm sorry it happened, because I'm not. Be happy with your Frenchman.'

As she tore the letter into little shreds, she was conscious of Clive's sympathetic gaze, like a devoted spaniel, she thought.

'Don't look like that!' she snapped. 'There's no need. Drew says it was all a mistake, and it was. I should never have listened to you in the first place. I must have been mad to come here.'

Clive put his hand on her arm.

'I'm sorry. I thought it would work out.'

'Well, it didn't, did it? It was all a big joke to him, and now Maxine has him back.'

'You do care for him,' Clive asserted.

Angry tears sprang to her eyes.

'I don't—I don't. I don't care if I never see him again. In fact I never am going to see him again. Can you be ready to take me to the coach in half an hour Clive? I want to be out of here before they return.'

The clothes she had worn yesterday had been washed and ironed while she slept, but she went to the camp shop and managed to buy some toilet articles, a subtly patterned Indian skirt and a white shirt in cotton. There was nothing to pack because she had lost everything in the river. She felt curiously free without her Paris clothes. This done, she went back to the office where Clive was to make last-minute arrangements. But when she arrived there, she found he was busily engaged on the radio system. As she approached, she wondered what could have happened to disturb his usually calm manner.

'What?' he was saying. 'My God, where did this happen? I see. And are they much hurt?'

He listened intently for a few minutes, just making the occasional remark, and as Sara heard the crackling noise coming through the receiver, and the hurried tones of a voice that she could not decipher, she felt a coldness settle in the region of her heart.

'Better not move him yet. I'll radio the hospital straight away and maybe they can fly a doctor out by helicopter. In these conditions planes can't land on the airfield—it's a sea of mud. Oh, you don't think it' necessary? He has recovered consciousness? Very well I'll come myself. Just give me your exact position.'

The crackling and the anxious voice stopped and Clive turned to Sara.

'They've had an accident. Maxine is a damned fool when she's driving. She and Drew were in the front truck, and the rest of the helpers were following with the equipment, when she saw something she wanted to photograph and swerved off into the veld. The truck hit an ant bear's hole and Drew was flung up against the roof. He wasn't wearing a seat-belt—I guess he didn't think he needed it. He must have taken a hell of a crack, because he was knocked unconscious, but he's recovered a little, apparently. I wanted to arrange for a doctor to be flown here, but Maxine doesn't seem to think it's necessary. However, I'll decide about it when I've seen him myself. I'm afraid I'll have to let you down, Sara. I'll arrange for someone else to drive you to the coach. I feel I must go to Drew.'

'I'm going with you, Clive,' Sara said urgently.

Clive smiled at her.

'I thought you'd say that.'

'He probably wouldn't want me there, but I'm going nevertheless. How's Maxine?,' she asked belatedly.

'Right as rain. She came through without a scratch. In fact she says she's leaving Drew in the care of one of the crew and is going on with the rest. She says the light is too good to waste this morning.'

'She's really incredible!' said Sara. 'I suppose the fact that she doesn't flap about things is a sign that she would make a good wilderness wife.'

'Well, personally, I'd need a woman a bit softer than Maxine,' said Clive.

'You might, but she seems to suit Drew.'

'I wonder.'

As she and Clive drove over the muddy roads, Sara felt a mounting anxiety about Drew. How could they believe Maxine when she said Drew was not badly hurt? She was so casual in her approach. Imagine going off and leaving him so she could take more photographs!

'The birds are coming back,' Clive commented as they drove by a place that was almost a lake now, and Sara saw a flock of flamingoes flying towards it, their necks long and stretched in straight lines, their undersides a rosy contrast to the black of some of their feathers. Red and yellow bishop birds hopped merrily around the reeds where before there had been hardly any sign of life. Normally she would have been thrilled and delighted with these new sights, but now there seemed to be a heavy lump of lead somewhere where her heart had been.

'Do you think Maxine was not telling you the truth

when she said he wasn't much hurt?' she asked Clive. 'I don't trust her. Could be she was being optimistic because she wanted to go on with her photography.'

'We'll know soon enough. The trucks are connected by radio. If we find he needs it I can send for a doctor straight away. We won't have lost much time.'

Sara felt she could not agree. If Drew were really hurt, and it sounded bad that he had been unconscious, any loss of time might be bad for him. At last they reached the place where the truck was standing, heeled over at an awkward angle some yards from the road. As soon as the car stopped, Sara was out of it and running towards the truck. A young man came towards them and she recognised one of Maxine's helpers.

'Thank God you have come!' the young man exclaimed. 'He doesn't look too good. Maxine insisted he was all right, but I'm not so sure.'

They had taken the seat out of the truck and Drew was lying on it in the scanty shade of a thorn tree. His head had been roughly bandaged, but blood had seeped through and the mopane bees were flying around his head. He looked dazed and hardly seemed to recognise them.

'Good God, we can't let him stay here!' exclaimed Clive 'I'll radio straight away for a doctor. Maxine must have been crazy to leave him like this! We must get him back to the camp. I'll drive very carefully.'

The next hour was an experience that sometimes haunted Sara's dreams. She sat in the back of the truck with Drew lying half conscious beside her. She tried to keep his head steady as the truck went over the bumps, for however carefully Clive was trying to drive, he could not always avoid the roughness of the roads.

It was a nightmare journey, and the worst thing was that she seemed to have no communication with Drew. He was conscious, she thought. At least, his eyes were open and every now and again he seemed to want to talk, but she could not understand what he was trying to say. But at last they were back at the camp and she and Clive got him to bed.

'The doctor should be here soon,' Clive said. 'They managed to get a helicopter, so he can land in the camp.'

Sara sat with Drew. His eyes were closed and she did not know whether he was aware that she was there. She held his hand because it seemed to give her some kind of communication with him, and it was as if she were trying to send some of her own strength through those long slender brown fingers that had given her so much joy.

I love him, she thought. I wouldn't admit it before, but now I know. It's hopeless. Too much has happened and he doesn't love me, but I know I can never get over him, never love anyone else.

At last the doctor arrived, and Sara went out of the room while he examined Drew. He seemed to be there for a very long time and she felt she could hardly stand the anxiety that she felt now.

'Is it bad?' she asked now as he and Clive came out of the room.

'It could have been much worse,' said the doctor. 'He's had a nasty bang, but he should be better in a few days time.'

'He doesn't seem to know me,' she said anxiously. 'He seems to be so dazed.'

'That will soon pass. You must understand, Mrs Mannion, that he's had a severe shock, but he has a very strong constitution and he'll get over it. He needs rest and quiet for a while, and what better place to find it than in this beautiful reserve?'

It had given Sara a surprise to be called by her married name. Clive must have told him that she was Drew's wife.

'He mustn't have any worry,' the doctor went on. 'Just keep him happy and you'll see he'll be his old self in a little while—but I'm sure you know how to do that, Mrs Mannion.'

'I'm going to stay,' she told Clive. 'It seems he needs me even if he doesn't know it.'

'Of course you're going to stay, and I'm going to

arrange to have a bed brought in for you. You must be near him.'

For the next few days, Sara stayed with Drew almost all the time except when Clive relieved her. Maxine had declared when she came back that she must go away now to arrange about the publication of her photographs. Now that she had taken those of the wet season, she had everything she required. She expressed very little anxiety about Drew.

'I'm sure he'll be all right,' she told Sara. 'Rather you than me. I'd be no good as a nurse.'

Sara felt worried sometimes because Drew seemed to spend his whole time sleeping and, although he accepted her ministrations, he did not seem to recognise her and hardly spoke to her.

Then one day, as she was bending over him, he opened his eyes, and now there was in them an expression she recognised.

'Sara, how good to see you! What are you doing here? How beautiful you look.'

She felt deeply thrilled by the tone of his voice, but was he still dreaming?

'Your hair is still that same lovely colour,' he went on. 'No one else has ever had hair the colour of yours— pure, pure gold, shining gold silk. And your eyes—I've never forgotten that deep violet blue. Oh, Sara, it's good to be able to see you again!'

'But Drew . . .' Sara felt puzzled. Was he still in a daze? Was he speaking about her colouring from memory or could he truly see her now? 'Drew, can you really see the colour of my hair and eyes?'

'Of course. Why not?'

'But you weren't able to see colour before.'

He frowned as if trying to concentrate.

'No, nor was I. But now I can. Oh, Sara, it's come back! My sight has come back. Good Lord, I can see the blue of the sky outside the window, I can see the reds in that rug—it isn't black and grey any more. But what's happened to me? I remember now. You've been looking after me. There was something happened to the truck. How long have I been like this?'

'For a few days. You got a bad bang on the head when Maxine drove into an ant-bear hole. Oh, Drew, are you really feeling all right?'

'I feel fine. A bit woozy, maybe. I remember now. Maxine has the damnedest way of driving. I must have hit the roof.'

'But can you really see?' asked Sara anxiously.

'It seems so. Coming to think of it, that specialist did tell me about some rare case where a man regained the use of the optic nerve when he'd had a bang on the head. It seems Maxine's crazy driving must have done me a good turn. Where is she, by the way?' Drew added.

'She's gone to fix up about the publication of her photographs.'

Sara felt a stab of jealousy. She had cared for Drew all these anxious days, and the first one he asked for was Maxine!

'Just as well. I think she'd been here long enough. She'll probably produce a very profitable book, but in spite of that, she never got the true feel of the wilderness. But, Sara, tell me, what are you doing here still? I thought you intended to go back the day I had the accident.'

'I was going, but I stayed.'

'To look after me? Oh, Sara, what trouble I seem to have caused you!'

'No trouble,' she assured him. 'I phoned Madame and told her I'd been delayed. She's furious, of course, but there's not much she can do about it.'

There was—quite a lot. Madame had threatened that, if Sara did not return immediately, she would have to find a replacement, but she did not tell Drew this.

'But you aren't going back. You wouldn't leave me now.'

There was a tenderness in his voice that she had not heard for years. She dared not believe what his eyes seemed to convey.

'I love you, Sara,' he said. 'I've always loved you. I

was a fool ever to let you go, but I knew you hated the wilderness and now I suppose, after the way I treated you, you've learned to hate me.'

She took his hand and caressed his long fingers.

'I could never hate you, Drew. I've loved you all these years—I know that now. I lied to you about having a French lover. There's never been anyone else but you.'

'My lovely Sara! I love you dearly, but what are we to do about us? You hate the wilderness and I could never live in a town. I thought I knew you would never stay here, and that's why I decided to kidnap you. I had hoped that those few days would effect some miraculous change, but then I realised I'd been too hopeful.'

'No, Drew, that's not true,' Sara assured him. 'I told you I hated the wilderness because I was angry with you at the time, but it's not right. I've come to see how you feel about it. It could be home to me. I'm no longer afraid.'

'Oh, Sara, lovely Sara, between us we've made a miracle. Do you really feel that you could live this kind of life now and not regret it?'

'No regrets,' said Sara. 'As long as I can be in your arms!'

'Now and for ever.'

'The doctor said you must rest and not get excited,' she warned.

'To hell with the doctor,' said Drew.

Coming Next Month in Harlequin Romances!

2737 RETURN TO WALLABY CREEK Kerry Allyne
The one man capable of running her father's Outback station and
saving a young woman's inheritance seems to despise her. So why
does he accept her marriage proposal?

2738 TO CAGE A WHIRLWIND Jane Donnelly
A native islander returns home when her brother is caught
pilfering from the new laird. She hates being taken as the mistress
of Calla—until she meets the laird's prospective bride!

2739 THE TROUBLE WITH BRIDGES Emma Goldrick
Every article a New England reporter writes about the engineer
the town hired to fix the old bridge makes him look foolish. But
what has her bias to do with love?

2740 AIR OF ENCHANTMENT Sarah Keene
A Los Angeles day-care teacher takes on an architect's visiting
niece and finds herself falling under the spell of her employer—an
amateur magician, graced in the art of illusion.

2741 MAGIC IN VIENNA Betty Neels
To an English governess, Vienna would be more appealing if her
host would stop burying his head in medical studies and show her
the true magic to be found in Vienna.

2742 WILD JASMINE Yvonne Whittal
With degree in hand, a graduate returns to Bombay to join her
father's firm, never expecting to be met by a rival architect. But
when tragedy strikes, their fates are bound together....

Author JOCELYN HALEY,
also known by her fans as SANDRA FIELD and JAN MACLEAN, now presents her eighteenth compelling novel.

DREAM OF DARKNESS

With the help of the enigmatic Bryce Sanderson, Kate MacIntyre begins her search for the meaning behind the nightmare that has haunted her since childhood.

Together they will unlock the past and forge a future.

Available at your favorite retail outlet in NOVEMBER.

The final book
in the trilogy by
MAURA SEGER

EDGE OF DAWN

The story of the Callahans and Garganos
concludes as Matthew and Tessa must stand
together against the forces that threaten to
destroy everything their families have built.

From the unrest and upheaval of the sixties
and seventies to the present, *Edge of Dawn*
explores a generation's coming of age
through the eyes of a man and a woman
determined to love no matter what the cost.

COMING IN FEBRUARY 1986

EDG-H-1

Take 4 best-selling love stories FREE
Plus get a FREE surprise gift!

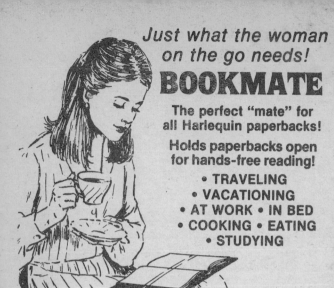